Fate's End

DS Maddy Frost - Book One

A Whitby Crime Thriller

Nic Roberts

Col Strebb

Copyright © 2025
by Nic Roberts & Col Strebb

'Fate's End'

All rights reserved.
No part of this book may be reproduced in any form or by any electronic or mechanical means, including information storage and retrieval systems, without written permission from the author, except for the use of brief quotations in a book review.
This is a work of fiction. Names, characters, places and incidents either are the product of the author's imagination or are used fictitiously. Some may be used for parody purposes.

Any resemblance to events, locales, business establishments, or actual persons living or dead is purely coincidental.

Love to read Detective Thrillers?

Join my Newsletter to be the first to hear about New Releases

http://eepurl.com/hskzML

Daniel shifted his kit bag on his shoulder and studied the car with controlled calm. He noticed the details others might miss. The way the vehicle leaned against the barrier, with steam rising from the engine, the rainwater mixing with blood on the ground, and the faint drip from a fractured radiator.

"Female driver, mid-twenties," a young officer said as he jogged up. "Car hit the barrier and flipped. She's alive, but barely." His voice carried urgency, his eyes darting between Daniel and the car as if waiting for a miracle.

But this wasn't a place for miracles, was it? Daniel nodded, eyes locked on the vehicle. He thrived on the urgency of these moments. Every decision mattered. It was the only time he felt in control, when the world narrowed to a single point of focus and nothing else intruded.

He crouched by the driver's side. The window had shattered into jagged edges, glass still clinging to the frame. Rain tapped against the twisted shell, running in rivulets down the panels. He leaned inside, pushing aside hanging wires and scraps of trim.

"We've got a pulse," he called out. His voice was steady; his gloved hands moved with precision. Blood streaked the woman's face, pooling under her temple. Her chest rose shallowly, with a faint wheeze between her lips. Her eyes fluttered once, then stilled.

"Oxygen," he ordered. A colleague handed him a mask. He worked fast, noting her leg fracture, the sound of her breathing, and the faint perfume beneath the smell of blood. He ignored her engagement ring and any details that might slow him down. They were distractions, things that pulled others off course.

The woman was young. Too young. A flicker of emotion stirred, but he forced it down. Compassion clouded judgement. He didn't have space for it here.

For a second, his wife's accident cut through his mind.

Prologue

The wreckage was spread across the wet road, a tangled mess of metal and glass lit by the flash of red and blue lights.

The car's bonnet crushed, the driver's side door folded inward, and the frame bent so far it was almost unrecognisable as a vehicle. Shards of glass scattered across the tarmac, reflecting the scene in broken slivers. A trail of engine oil and blood led away from the vehicle, pooling in a dark puddle under the street lights. The air bit with the acrid tang of burnt rubber, leaking fuel and something much more human. Radios crackled, officers shouted to each other, and sirens wailed in the distance. The entire scene felt tense, every person present working against the clock.

Daniel Cross stepped onto the scene, his boots crunching over the debris. In his early fifties, with close-cropped greying hair and a wiry build that spoke of years on the job, he had the kind of weathered face that inspired immediate confidence in a crisis. The cold wind cut across his uniform and carried the voices of bystanders standing behind the police tape. A few whispered to each other, phones in hand, their faces pale.

Her pale face.

Her lifeless eyes.

The moment he'd realised there was nothing left to save.

Daniel forced the memory aside and steadied his hands as he adjusted the mask. That crash had been chaos, beyond his control. The helplessness had been unbearable. Not this time. Here he could act.

"We need to clear her airway," he said. The woman coughed faintly. Her pulse stayed weak but steady. He gave a small nod. She'd live, for now.

They worked quickly. Firefighters stabilised the car with a hydraulic ram, pushing against the frame to hold it steady. Another forced open the passenger door with cutters, sparks flying as the metal gave way. Daniel guided them, his instructions sharp and precise. "Hold her head steady." A neck brace was secured, a backboard slid into place. On Daniel's count, the team lifted her, setting her on the stretcher with care, their boots slipping slightly on the slick surface.

Strapped down under the sheet, she looked fragile.

But everyone does when they're on a stretcher, don't they? Daniel thought as they wheeled her to the ambulance, Daniel cast one last glance at the twisted shell of the car. For now, she was safe.

As the rush eased, Daniel leaned against the ambulance, watching the remnants of the scene. The woman was stabilised and handed over to surgeons at the hospital. The road grew quieter. Cones, wrappers, and broken glass were scattered across the wet surface. Emergency crews began to leave. The sound of rain replaced the shouts and machinery, and the blue lights dimmed one by one as vehicles pulled away.

Daniel stood still. He didn't feel triumph. Survival wasn't always a victory. "She should have died tonight," he muttered, folding his arms.

But fate isn't finished with her yet. The night still had a long way to go yet, before it was done.

Daniel looked at the wreckage one last time before heading back, his expression blank to anyone watching. Days later, sitting in his flat, the news confirmed what he'd been waiting for. The woman had died overnight, as her condition had worsened without warning. The report was brief, then moved on to the next story. No one lingered on her name.

Daniel leaned back in his chair, fingers pressed together. "Fate always wins," he whispered.

He allowed himself a moment to take in the certainty of it, his eyes fixed on his reflection in the black screen of the television. He was the only one who understood what it meant.

Others shouldn't have the second chances Sarah never got.

Chapter One

The mist clung to Whitby like an overprotective parent, smothering the cobbled streets and crumbling cliffs. The distant cry of gulls, mingled with the faint roar of the North Sea, made the town feel alive in its own unsettling way. Detective Sergeant Madeline Frost rolled her suitcase over the uneven pavement, her boots clacking in the eerie quiet, the sound swallowed by the thick fog that blurred the edges of her hometown.

"Home sweet home," she muttered bitterly under her breath. The weight of her return sat heavy on her chest, a nagging reminder of everything she'd hoped to leave behind when she'd first left.

But here I am, she thought sourly, back where it all began, hoping that the shadows of her past wouldn't swallow her whole.

The cottage she'd grown up in loomed ahead, its white-washed walls dampened by the perpetual drizzle. Her mother's meticulously maintained window boxes, once full of flowers, were now mostly weeds. The soft glow of a porch light spilled onto the stone step as the door opened before she could knock.

"You're late," Her mother, Claire Frost, announced, tea

towel slung over one shoulder. Her hair, streaked with silver, was tied back in the same messy bun she'd always worn.

Maddy raised an eyebrow, tilting her head as if to gauge her mother's mood. "Nice to see you too, Mam."

"Did the big city swallow you whole?" Claire asked with a smile, ignoring the sarcasm and ushered her inside. The scent of fresh bread and lavender polish hit Maddy the moment she crossed the threshold, a sensory time capsule of her childhood.

"No, but it tried to," Maddy replied, leaning in for a brief hug. "Miss me?"

Her mother's eyes warmed, though her words remained teasing. "Hardly. But the spiders and cobwebs in your old room will be *thrilled*."

Maddy smirked, dragging her suitcase down the narrow hallway. It was almost comforting how little had changed. That same creaky floorboard. The same mismatched chairs around the kitchen table. Even the crack in the plaster by the pantry remained, its jagged line as familiar as an old friend.

They sat in the kitchen, mugs of tea steaming between them. The warm light cast a soft glow over Claire's lined face, her gaze heavy with unspoken thoughts. Her lips pursed in the way they always did when she had something to say but hadn't yet decided how to say it.

"So, how long are you staying?" Claire finally asked, cutting straight to the point.

"I'm not sure," Maddy admitted, wrapping her hands around the mug for warmth. "It depends on how things go with work."

Claire's eyebrows lifted. "Low-stress transfer, they called it? In this town?"

Maddy's laugh was short and bitter. "Low-stress compared to the city, at least. No drug lords, county lines or high-speed chases here, right?"

"Just damp socks and stubborn fishermen," Claire quipped, her lips twitching into the faintest smile.

The silence that followed was companionable but tinged with something heavier. Maddy's eyes flicked to the steam rising from her mug, her fingers tightening slightly around the handle. Burnout was an ugly word, but it fit. The last case she'd worked in the city had been the kind that burrowed under your skin and stayed there, whispering in the quiet moments.

If she looked back on her time in the city, she realised she'd spent her time there running herself ragged, chasing criminals, losing sleep, and pouring every ounce of herself into a system that seemed designed to wear people down. Even the people employed to protect it. Coming back to Whitby was supposed to be her reset button, though so far, it felt more like a pause screen on an anxiety-riddled video game.

Maddy looked up at her mother, who was quietly watching her over the rim of her mug.

"You don't look like you've slept properly in weeks," Claire said, her tone softened by concern.

"That's because I haven't," Maddy gave a small shrug. She forced a smile, but it didn't reach her eyes. "You'd think organising a transfer back to a quiet little seaside town would come with less baggage, right?" She laughed faintly, though it sounded hollow even to her.

Maddy's hands fidgeted against the mug as her thoughts wandered. The weight of her failures gnawed at her, the cases she hadn't solved, and the lives she hadn't been able to save. Those faces haunted her more than she cared to admit, creeping into her dreams when she finally managed to sleep. She felt like she was running on fumes, trying to convince herself she had more to give when, deep down, she wasn't so sure.

Her mother sighed a little, but she didn't press further. Instead, she handed Maddy another biscuit, the Frost ceremonial gesture of a quiet truce. It was a small comfort, but in that moment, Maddy thought it was more than she deserved.

Maddy's phone buzzed just as she was contemplating whether a third biscuit was worth the judgmental look she'd get from her mother. She glanced at the screen: DI Alan Harper. She sighed and answered.

"Hello?"

"Heard you came back for a simpler life?" Harper's gravelly voice carried through the line. "I need you at the station. Dead fisherman. Not as glamorous as city crime, but it'll do."

The voice was unmistakable. Harper had been her first supervisor when she'd started at Whitby station, back when he was still a sergeant. Gruff, demanding, but never unfair. She'd learned more from him in those early years than she had in all her training. The promotion to DI suited him.

Maddy rolled her eyes, already reaching for her coat. "You really know how to sell it, sir."

"It's a gift. Be here in fifteen." The line clicked dead.

"Let me guess," Claire said, sipping her tea, her eyes flicking briefly toward the rain-speckled window. The faint creak of the house settling filled the momentary silence. "Crime waits for no man."

Maddy glanced around the kitchen as she peeled her coat off the chair back, her gaze lingering on the faded wallpaper that her mother still hadn't changed. The same small shelf above the sink held the same dusty collection of trinkets: a chipped porcelain cat, a miniature lighthouse, and a faded photograph of her father holding a young Maddy at the beach. The weight of the past pressed on her chest suddenly.

"You've still got it," Maddy replied, forcing a smile as she threaded her arms through her jacket sleeves. "The detective instincts, I mean. You'd give Harper a run for his money."

Claire snorted softly, a flicker of amusement breaking

through her usual guarded expression. "Don't flatter me, Maddy. You're the one who gets to chase ghosts around this town now. Just you promise me you won't let them catch you."

Believe me, I don't want them to, Maddy thought as she made her way out the door.

The Whitby station was a modest building, its brick façade weathered by decades of salt and storms. A slightly crooked sign above the door bore the faded crest of the North Yorkshire Police. Maddy hesitated at the entrance, her gaze lingering on the uneven pavement beneath her feet before she pushed through the heavy door.

Inside, the station smelled faintly of disinfectant and strong coffee. *Just like it used to,* she thought. The walls were adorned with community notices and outdated posters warning against petty crimes. A bulletin board near the entrance displayed a mix of local announcements and fading newspaper clippings about minor cases solved long ago. The muted hum of fluorescent lights added to the sense of utilitarian drabness.

An older sergeant with a stern expression manned the main desk, though he barely glanced up as Maddy walked past. The station had the kind of functional clutter that spoke of a team stretched thin, piles of paperwork stacked precariously on desks, half-empty mugs scattered across surfaces, and a radio crackling faintly in the background. Maddy barely had time to take it all in before a young officer bounded toward her, her steps brisk and energetic.

"DS Frost, right?" The woman extended a hand, her smile bright and slightly nervous. She was in her late twenties, with dark hair pulled back in a practical ponytail and warm brown eyes that radiated genuine enthusiasm.

"Call me Maddy," she responded, shaking her hand firmly. "You're the welcoming committee?"

"DC Emily Ward, at your service," the woman laughed, almost bouncing on her toes.

"Please tell me you're this chipper *after* coffee, not before," Maddy said, grinning despite herself.

"Oh, it gets worse," Emily said with a wink, motioning for Maddy to follow.

In the briefing room, DI Harper himself leaned against the table, a thin file in hand. He was a bear of a man, promoted since she'd been away, with a greying beard and a permanent scowl that somehow managed to look affectionate when aimed at the right people.

"Frost," he greeted, nodding. "Welcome back to Whitby. Hope you've missed damp cottages and seaside murder."

"Love them both," Maddy said dryly. "What have we got?"

He slid the file across the table. "Andy Pearson. Local fisherman. Survived a boat collapse last week. Found dead in his sleep yesterday. No obvious cause."

Maddy flipped through the pages, her brow furrowing as she read the report. Did she remember Andy Pearson before? His name didn't ring a bell. But had he been one of the many nameless locals that Maddy had passed through Whitby High Street? Or queued behind in the supermarket?

That was the thing about death, she felt a morbid shudder run down her spine. Death was always out there, always waiting around the corner, ready to pounce.

"Lucky enough to survive the sea, unlucky enough to lose the lottery of life," she mumbled, then paused, her gaze lingering on the autopsy summary.

"Anything stand out?" Harper asked, watching her with a mix of curiosity and expectation.

"No obvious signs of trauma," Maddy read slowly, tapping

her fingers against the edge of the file. "Heart failure? Poisoning? Could be natural causes, but..."

Harper snorted. "Come on, Frost. You were never someone who believed in coincidence."

She smirked faintly but didn't respond. Instead, she flipped back to the section detailing Andy Pearson's near-death experience. "The boat collapse. How bad was it?"

"Bad enough," Harper said. "Two others went down with the wreckage. Andy was the only survivor. Local papers called him 'Lucky Pearson'." His tone carried a hint of disdain for the nickname.

Maddy's expression darkened. "Lucky until he wasn't, I guess." She closed the file with a sharp snap. Her mind raced through possibilities, each one more troubling than the last. "I'll know more once I see the scene."

Harper grunted. "Exactly. Go have a look. Ward will go with you."

* * *

The fishing cottage was as unremarkable as they came, a squat, weather-beaten structure nestled against the rising cliffs, its wooden slats warped from years of Whitby weather. Tangled nets and rusting lobster pots were piled haphazardly against the walls, their edges frayed from use. The scent of salt and decay permeated the air, mingling with a faint, sour chemical smell that set Maddy's teeth on edge. The windows were streaked with grime, filtering the grey daylight into murky shadows as the officers stepped inside.

The air in the cramped bedroom felt heavier, almost oppressive. Maddy's boots creaked against the uneven floorboards as she stepped further in, her eyes scanning every detail. A narrow bed dominated the space, its sheets rumpled and bunched, as though someone had tossed and turned violently in their last moments. On the nightstand sat an empty pill bottle, the label partially smudged with moisture. Next to it, a framed photo of Andy Pearson grinned back at her, the fisherman holding a monstrous catch, his weathered face radiating pride and weariness.

The faint hum of a dripping tap echoed from the adjoining kitchenette, and the peeling paint revealed layers of neglect. A single light bulb hung from the ceiling, its weak glow casting uneven shadows that danced with every slight breeze. It felt as though the room itself was holding its breath, waiting for someone to notice what it was hiding.

"Doesn't scream foul play," Emily said from the doorway, her voice soft but curious.

"No, it doesn't," Maddy replied, though her gut told her otherwise.

Sometimes they don't scream, she thought. *Sometimes the murder scenes whisper.*

Maddy crouched by the nightstand, picking up the empty bottle. Sleeping pills. Normal enough, but something about it felt off. She couldn't place it yet.

She turned to Emily. "Who found him?"

"Neighbour," Emily said. "Didn't see him leave for his morning haul and got worried. Came by and found him like this."

Maddy frowned, her gaze drifting back to the bed. Something wasn't right. The way the sheets were tangled. The faint smell of something chemical beneath the salt air. It was subtle, but it was there, an undercurrent of wrongness that her instincts latched onto.

"What are you thinking?" Emily asked, her voice even quieter now.

Maddy straightened, placing the pill bottle back on the

nightstand. Her gut churned as her eyes swept the room again, catching details that seemed to amplify her unease. The faint chemical smell lingering beneath the salt air was sharper now, acrid and wrong, as though something had seeped into the very fabric of the place. The tangled sheets on the bed looked more than disturbed; they bore the chaotic impression of a restless, frantic struggle. The photo of Andy on the nightstand, once an image of triumph, now seemed almost mocking in its placement beside the empty bottle. Her thoughts raced, piecing together the subtle discord.

"Why was the pill bottle empty but still here?" she murmured, almost to herself. "If he had used it up, he would throw it in that, would he?" She pointed at the small round bin by the nightstand, empty of anything.

The air in the room felt heavier, like it was closing in. Her gut churned again, the first flicker of unease settling deep, more profound with each passing second.

"I'm thinking this doesn't feel like an accident," she said, her tone heavy with certainty. She turned toward Emily, her eyes sharp.

"And I hate being right."

Chapter Two

Maddy tapped her pen against the desk as she read through Andy Pearson's account of the boat collapse. It was concise, almost mechanical in detail, but the key point stood out. Andy's life had been saved (for a short while, at least) by Daniel Cross, the lead paramedic who'd pulled him from the wreckage. His name appeared again and again in the reports, like a watermark she couldn't ignore.

"Daniel Cross," she said more to herself, underlining the name. "Our hero paramedic."

Emily looked up from sorting through a stack of files. "You've heard of him, right? Everyone in town has. He's practically a legend. Saved countless lives over the years, not just Andy Pearson's. Fires, car crashes, boating accidents... You name it, he's been there; pulling men from the icy water half-drowned. There's even talk of him volunteering his time at the hospice when he's not on call. Parents call him a miracle worker."

"I'm getting that impression," Maddy replied dryly. "Harper mentioned he's showered with thank-you cards and biscuits."

Emily laughed. "It's true. My mam sent him a fruitcake last Christmas when he helped her neighbour after a fall."

Maddy leaned back in her chair, her pen tapping a faster rhythm. "What do we know about him? Beyond the fruitcakes and heroics?" Her voice carried a faint edge of frustration.

People who made a habit of being in the right place at the right time often had their own reasons for doing so."

Or maybe I'm just being cynical, Maddy sighed, leaning back in her chair. Working in the city had a way of making you distrust everyone.

Emily hesitated, her brow furrowing. "Nothing bad, if that's what you're fishing for. He's respected. Everyone says he's got nerves of steel, like he was made for this kind of work."

"Too perfect," Maddy muttered under her breath, earning a curious glance from Emily. She closed the file with a snap and stood. "I'm going to ask around. See if our saintly paramedic has any cracks in his halo."

* * *

"Daniel? You mean the paramedic?" The woman behind the counter at the bait shop paused, her hands hovering over a pile of tangled nets. Her face, weathered by years of salt air and sun, softened into an expression of admiration. "He's a saint, that one. Saved Andy's life, you know."

Maddy leaned on the counter, feigning casual interest. "So I've heard," she kept her tone light, but probing. "Ever noticed anything... off about him?"

"Off?" The woman's brows knitted, her expression shifting to defensive. "Love, he's one of the good ones. Always first on the scene, calm under pressure. What are you implying?"

"Nothing," Maddy said quickly, lifting her hands in mock surrender. "Just trying to get a sense of who he is. Part of the job, you know." She offered a small smile, but the woman's narrowed eyes didn't waver.

"Well, if you're sniffing around him, you're barking up the wrong tree," the woman said firmly. "Daniel Cross has done more good for this town than most. You'd be better off catching whoever's been nicking lobster pots." She turned her attention back to the nets, effectively ending the conversation.

Maddy thanked her and stepped out of the shop, into the crisp afternoon air. Her boots crunched against the gravel as she glanced up at the overcast sky, the mist softening the edges of the town. Whitby's residents were fiercely protective of their own, she'd learned that the hard way as a teenager. But something about Daniel Cross' spotless reputation didn't sit right. People this perfect usually had skeletons rattling somewhere.

Her phone buzzed in her pocket. It was a message from Emily: *Back at the station. Harper's grumbling. Again.* Maddy smirked and typed a quick reply: *He'd grumble at sunshine.* Stuffing the phone back into her jacket, she headed back for the station.

* * *

"Let me get this straight," Harper said, leaning back in his chair with a groan. His office was as cluttered as the rest of the station, papers stacked in precarious piles on every available surface. "You want to question the paramedic who saved Andy Pearson? The same guy who gets showered with thank-you cards and biscuits every year?"

"Maybe he likes biscuits too much," Maddy quipped, tossing a report onto his desk. "He saved Andy's life, then Andy ends up dead days later. That doesn't feel like coincidence to me."

"Coincidence is how small towns survive, Frost," Harper

muttered, rubbing his temples. "If you start pulling threads, the whole bloody tapestry unravels."

Emily, perched on the edge of a nearby desk, chimed in. "I mean, he's practically a local hero. It'll ruffle feathers if we go poking around."

Maddy crossed her arms. "I'm not saying we slap cuffs on him and march him through the square. I just want to talk to him. Quietly."

Harper sighed, his chair creaking under his weight. "Fine. But tread lightly. If you're wrong about this, it's your head."

"Wouldn't have it any other way," Maddy called over her shoulder, already heading for the door.

* * *

Maddy had called the ambulance station that morning, leaving a polite message asking if Daniel Cross could spare some time for a follow-up interview. She'd expected to wait days for a response. Instead, he'd texted within the hour: Happy to help. Outside your station at 3?

Daniel Cross was waiting outside the station, leaning casually against the ambulance with his arms crossed. His uniform was pristine, his posture relaxed. As Maddy approached, he smiled, the kind of smile that seemed too practised, too perfect.

"Detective Sergeant Frost," the paramedic said smoothly, extending a hand. "Pleasure to meet you."

"Likewise, Mr. Cross," Maddy replied, shaking his hand. His grip was firm but not overpowering, textbook polite. She noticed his eyes, though. Calm. Too calm. The kind of calm that came from someone who'd mastered control, both of himself and of how others saw him.

"I hear you've got some questions for me," he said, his tone almost playful.

"Just tying up loose ends," Maddy replied lightly. "Mind if we talk inside?"

He gestured toward the station with an easy nod. "Lead the way."

* * *

The interview room was small and unassuming, the kind of space designed to make people uncomfortable. Daniel Cross, however, seemed perfectly at ease as he took a seat across from Maddy. He rested his hands on the table, his fingers interlaced, his posture open.

"Andy was a good man," he began, his voice steady and measured. "He fought hard out there. We were lucky to get to him in time."

"Lucky," Maddy echoed, jotting down notes. "Do you find yourself getting lucky often, Mr. Cross? Seems you've been at the scene of a lot of close calls lately."

His smile didn't waver. "It's the nature of the job, Detective. When people call for help, we're there."

"Convenient," she muttered under her breath, then looked up. "And you didn't notice anything unusual about Andy's condition after the rescue?"

"Nothing that stood out," Daniel replied smoothly. "He was shaken, of course. Who wouldn't be after something like that? But physically, he was stable when we left him."

Maddy studied him, her pen hovering over her notebook. "Did you follow up with him?"

"Not directly," he said, tilting his head slightly. "We're often onto the next emergency before we have a chance to look back. But I'm sorry to hear he's gone. Truly."

He spoke with the ease of someone used to being believed. But Maddy noticed how his fingers tapped rhythmically against the side of the chair, a small crack in his otherwise unshakable composure. It wasn't much, but it was enough to keep her on edge.

"It must be difficult," she said, her tone softening slightly. "Being there for people in their worst moments."

"It has its challenges," Daniel admitted, his gaze steady. "But it's rewarding too, you know, knowing you've made a difference." He paused, a faint smile playing at his lips. "Though sometimes, it feels like fate has its own plans, doesn't it?"

Maddy tilted her head, her pen halting mid-tap. "Fate? Does someone in your job really believe in fate?"

"Don't you?" He leaned forward slightly, his voice dipping into a softer, almost conspiratorial tone. "Think about it. You're standing at a crossroads, seconds from disaster, and something intervenes. A red light stops your car. A bystander who steps in. Or a paramedic who happens to be passing by. Coincidence, sure. But fate?" He let the word hang in the air like a challenge.

Maddy didn't answer immediately, her instincts prickling. She leaned back in her chair, keeping her expression neutral. "I think we make our own luck."

Daniel chuckled, shaking his head as if amused by her response. "Maybe. Or maybe some people aren't meant to cheat it."

Her brow furrowed at the odd phrasing, but she pushed it aside. "Thank you for your time, Mr. Cross," she said, closing her notebook with a decisive snap. "I'll be in touch if I need anything else."

He stood gracefully, his movements fluid, and offered another handshake. "Anytime, Detective. Happy to help."

As he reached the door, he hesitated, glancing back over his shoulder. "It's funny, though," he said, his tone light, yet Maddy was sure she could detect something sharper underneath. "How close we all come to death, every single day. Some people get second chances. Others...don't."

The words hung in the air long after he left, the faint creak of the closing door breaking the spell. Maddy sat frozen for a moment, her mind replaying his parting comment. It wasn't what he'd said, exactly. It was how he'd said it, like someone who understood the rules of a game no one else could see.

Her pen resumed its rhythmic tapping against the desk as she opened her book and stared at her notes, her gut whispering the same thing it always did when something didn't add up: *Dig deeper*.

Chapter Three

Maddy leaned against the station wall, her breath pooling in the chilly morning air. The rough, cold bricks pressed through her coat, grounding her as she stared at the grey horizon. Daniel Cross' words remained looped in her mind like a bad song lyric, and each repetition twisting her stomach a little tighter.

"Fate has a way of balancing things out."

Was it just a philosophical throwaway line, or something darker? Were all paramedics amateur mystics, or just Whitby's?

She rubbed her hands together, trying to shake off the tension. His calm, his unnerving ability to say so much without really saying anything, still crawled under her skin. He wasn't just too polished; he was also too deliberate, like every word had been rehearsed. Her gut told her to keep digging, but gut feelings didn't count for much without evidence. And so far, she had nothing but a nagging sense that he knew more than he let on.

Her phone buzzed in her pocket. With a sigh, she pulled it out and saw Harper's name flashing on the screen. She swiped to answer. "Frost."

"Got another one for you," Harper said without preamble. She could hear papers rustling in the background. "Tourist. Sophie Chambers. Found dead in her hotel room this morning."

Maddy straightened, a sharp chill slicing through her that had nothing to do with the cold.

"Sophie Chambers," she repeated, the name ringing in her memory. An incident report? Or some local gossip?

"I know that name from somewhere," she said.

"You should do. Nearly drowned last week at high tide," Harper said, his tone flat. "And guess who pulled her out?"

"Daniel Cross," Maddy muttered, her stomach twisting again.

"Yep. I've sent Emily ahead to secure the scene. Get over there."

* * *

The Resolution Hotel was one of Whitby's nicer establishments, perched on a quiet side street with a view of the harbour. Its faded elegance fit the town; quaint but worn, with hints of former grandeur.

Maddy stepped into the lobby, the scent of polished wood and lavender clinging to the air. A thin, wiry man in an ill-fitting suit hovered near the reception desk, wringing his hands nervously. His name tag read *Mr. Hargrove*.

"Detective Sergeant Frost," Maddy said, flashing her badge. "Are you the manager?"

"Yes, Detective," he stammered, wiping his hands on his trousers. "Terrible tragedy, just terrible. Seemed a lovely young woman."

"Did she have any visitors?" Maddy asked, pulling out her notebook.

"No one. Kept to herself mostly. Quiet as a mouse." He hesitated, glancing toward the stairs. "Though she did seem a little...jumpy. Asked for extra locks on her door."

Maddy's pen stilled mid-note. "Extra locks?"

"Said she wanted to feel safe," he said with a shrug. "I didn't ask questions. It's my place to meet my guests needs as best I can, no matter how bizarre some of them might seem to me."

Maddy nodded, tucking her notebook away. "I'll need to see her room."

The room was quiet, almost eerily so, Maddy thought as she stepped inside. The faint scent of lavender lingered, clashing with the sterility of death that hung in the air. Sophie's belongings were meticulously arranged, a suitcase tucked neatly in the corner, a book left open on the bedside table. It was too tidy, too composed, as if someone had deliberately erased any sign of chaos.

Maddy crouched by the bed, her gaze scanning every detail. The duvet was pulled back, a corner untouched, suggesting Sophie had lain down and never gotten back up. Her pale face was tilted slightly to the side, eyes half-closed as if she had simply drifted off. A faint trace of lavender perfume clung to her skin, mingling with the colder, metallic undertone of death. Her hands rested loosely by her sides, unmarked and unbruised. There was a half-empty bottle of water on the night-stand, condensation beading along its surface. Maddy touched it lightly; it was still cool, as perhaps Sophie had taken a sip just before lying down for the last time.

"She didn't even struggle," Maddy thought aloud, her voice low. There were no signs of a fight, no overturned furniture or broken glass. Just a stillness that felt all wrong.

Emily appeared in the doorway, her face tight. "Patel's on his way; he'll spot anything we've missed."

Dr. Vishaal Patel, the coroner, was new to her but carried a reputation that preceded him. Colleagues had described him as meticulous, unflappable, and almost unnervingly clinical. He had a knack for spotting what others missed, dissecting details with a sharp, surgical precision. While Maddy appreciated his professionalism, she wondered how he might respond to a case as peculiar as Sophie's. If there was something to find here, Patel would likely uncover it, but she couldn't shake the feeling that his detached demeanour might clash with the gravity of this investigation.

Maddy nodded, standing and dusting her hands on her trousers. "What do we know about her?"

"Tourist from London. Thirty-two. Checked in last week after the drowning incident. Looks like she'd planned to stay through the weekend," Emily said, flipping through her notes. "No family in town. Just a few friends back home. I've already got someone trying to contact them."

Maddy crossed her arms, her gaze lingering on the bed. "And Daniel Cross? What's his story on the drowning?"

"Standard heroics," Emily said with a shrug. "Saw her struggling in the water, pulled her out, stabilised her until the ambulance arrived. Everyone at the beach called him a lifesaver."

"Of course they did," Maddy muttered.

* * *

By the time Dr. Vishaal Patel arrived, the room had taken on the sterile, methodical atmosphere of an investigation. Patel was brisk, flipping through his notes as he stood over Sophie's body. His sharp eyes scanned every detail, his expression giving nothing away.

"No signs of foul play," he said finally, snapping off his gloves and setting them neatly aside. "No obvious cause of death either. It's as if her body just... stopped."

Huh? Maddy thought. No cause of death and yet no foul play. *How did that work?*

Dr Patel gestured toward the faint discolouration of Sophie's lips. "No evidence of asphyxiation, no trauma. It's strange. Her vitals would suggest a perfectly healthy individual. The only anomaly is...well, nothing." He frowned, flipping through his notes again, almost as if he were hoping to find an error in his own meticulous process. "If it weren't for the fact that she's lying here, I'd argue there's no reason she should be dead at all."

Maddy frowned, stepping closer. "People don't just stop, Vishaal. What about the drowning incident?"

"Unrelated, as far as I can tell. There's no water in the lungs, though that's not definitive yet; I'll need to confirm under closer analysis. But from the initial inspection, there's no evidence of drowning or secondary complications from her earlier incident. Physically, she should have been fine." He hesitated, tapping a pen against his clipboard as though weighing his next words. "But the timing is peculiar, I'll give you that. A body this intact doesn't just stop without reason." He looked up, meeting Maddy's eyes. "Whatever caused this, it's not something obvious. We'll need a full tox screen and histology to rule out the less visible culprits."

Maddy exchanged a glance with Emily, who raised her eyebrows in silent agreement.

"Peculiar isn't good enough," Maddy said. "Keep digging."

* * *

Back at the station, Maddy and Emily sat across from each other, the desk between them cluttered with files and coffee cups. Emily leaned back in her chair, her arms crossed. "So, our guy Daniel has another coincidence to explain."

"Coincidence?" Maddy scoffed, pushing her coffee aside. "At this rate, he's going to need a lawyer, not biscuits."

Emily grinned. "I'll take biscuits over coincidences any day."

Maddy's pen drummed against the desk, her mind spinning. She let her eyes drift over the cluttered files scattered in front of her, the evidence bags lined up with grim precision. Sophie's file sat open, the photo clipped to the top staring up at her with an almost haunting stillness.

"I feel like I'm missing something," Maddy muttered. She reached for the file again, flipping through the pages for anything she might have missed. Her fingers brushed against the diary bagged for evidence, and she paused, her curiosity piqued.

"Let's dig into Sophie's background. Something doesn't add up."

* * *

Sophie's diary was small and leather-bound, its pages filled with neat, looping handwriting that spoke of someone meticulous, even in her thoughts. Maddy turned the pages carefully, her eyes scanning the words with growing unease.

"August 15th: Lucky to be alive.

August 16th: I can't shake the feeling someone's watching me."

The next few entries were mundane, mentions of quiet days spent wandering Whitby's streets, admiring the abbey, and trying to relax after the incident at the beach. But the tone shifted abruptly in the last entry, its words written with what looked like a slight tremor in the pen stroke.

"August 18th: I'm safe here. Aren't I?"

Emily leaned over her shoulder. "Paranoia?" she suggested.

Maddy's eyes lingered on the final entry. A chill ran down her spine, the words sinking into her like a weight. Safe. The word felt wrong, hollow. Sophie hadn't been safe. And now she never would be.

Maddy closed Sophie's diary with a soft snap, her fingers lingering on the cover as if the worn leather might yield another secret. She turned to Emily, and the weight of unanswered questions pressed heavily on her chest. "Why write something like that?" she said, almost to herself. "Why be afraid when you've just survived something so terrifying?"

Emily shrugged, but her brow furrowed. "Maybe the near-death experience left her paranoid. Or maybe she had a reason."

The station's faint hum of activity filtered through the room, grounding Maddy momentarily. She placed the diary back into the evidence bag, her mind buzzing with possibilities. Then, a vibration broke through the quiet. Her phone buzzed on the desk, jolting her thoughts. She picked it up, frowning at the screen.

Unknown number. *Wrong place. Wrong questions. Wrong move.*

Her breath hitched, her eyes narrowing as she stared at the message. Emily leaned closer. "What is it?"

Maddy set the phone down slowly, her jaw tightening. "Looks like someone doesn't want me digging."

Chapter Four

Maddy sat in the dimly lit corridor of the coroner's office, her face illuminated by the small square of her phone screen.

Wrong place. Wrong questions. Wrong move.

She stared at the message for the hundredth time, her jaw tightening with a mix of frustration and unease. Whoever had sent it clearly underestimated her. She wasn't about to stop digging, especially now.

Shoving the phone back into her pocket, Maddy paced the hallway outside Dr. Patel's office. The sterile scent of disinfectant clung to the air, and the faint hum of machinery buzzed through the walls. Patel's voice drifted faintly from inside, calm and measured as always. Maddy blew out a breath, trying to rein in her thoughts. The text had rattled her more than she wanted to admit.

"Detective Sergeant Frost," Patel's voice called from behind the door. "You can come in now."

* * *

Dr. Vishaal Patel stood over the stainless steel examination table, flipping through a clipboard with his usual meticulous focus. The room was brightly lit, its clinical sterility amplified by the stark white walls and the metallic sheen of cabinets housing sharp and gleaming precision tools. The body of Sophie Chambers lay in the centre of the room, shrouded by a thin white sheet that barely concealed the eerie stillness of death. The sharp tang of antiseptic lingered in the air, mingling with the faint hum of the nearby refrigeration units.

"No physical trauma, no toxins, no definitive cause of death," Patel began, his voice clipped and efficient, though there was a faint edge of curiosity beneath his usual detachment. He finally glanced at Maddy, his sharp eyes catching her gaze. "Same as Andy Pearson." He flipped a page on his clipboard, his fingers pausing momentarily as though something about the case unsettled him too.

Maddy's chair scraped against the floor as she pulled it closer to the table. She leaned forward, narrowing her eyes at the report in Patel's hands. "So, what killed them?"

Patel finally looked up, his expression unreadable. "If I had to guess? A switch just…flipped."

Maddy folded her arms, irritation creeping into her voice. "People don't just stop like that, Vishaal," Maddy said, her irritation bubbling to the surface. "We're not bloody robots. Something, someone, has to be triggering this."

"I don't make the rules, Detective. I just report the facts," Patel said, his tone almost dry. "And the facts here are decidedly odd. Physically, there's nothing that explains why Sophie Chambers or Andy Pearson are dead."

He gestured to Sophie's body, pulling back the sheet just enough to expose her face. Her features were serene, almost untouched by death, as though she'd simply fallen asleep. Patel tapped the clipboard with his pen. "No signs of asphyxiation, no cardiac issues, and no evidence of external interference. And yet..."

"And yet, she's lying here," Maddy finished grimly. "What about adrenaline levels? Could something have triggered a stress response?"

Patel hesitated. "Both Sophie and Andy showed elevated adrenaline postmortem. It's unusual, given the circumstances of their deaths."

"Unusual how?" Maddy pressed.

"It suggests they experienced significant stress right before they died, despite being at rest when it happened," Patel said, his gaze meeting hers. "It's certainly not definitive, but it raises questions about what could have caused that kind of physiological response."

"Or *who* could have caused it," Maddy muttered under her breath.

* * *

The walk back to her car was brisk, the cold wind cutting through her coat as she tried to piece together the fragments of evidence. Sophie's death wasn't just unusual. There was no doubt about that.

"You can't stop fate," she whispered under her breath, remembering her creepy conversation with Daniel Cross. His name loomed large in her mind, but she still lacked the thread to tie it all together. And then there was the text message...

Someone was watching her, trying to push her away or, worse, mislead her.

By the time Maddy reached home, the golden glow of the kitchen light spilled into the hallway, chasing away the gloom of the day. The rich scent of roasted vegetables and something savoury wafted toward her, wrapping her in a momentary cocoon of warmth. Claire was at the kitchen counter, her sleeves rolled up, chopping cucumbers and tomatoes with the kind of precise care only a retired schoolteacher could muster. The rhythmic sound of the knife against the cutting board was oddly soothing, filling the space with a sense of quiet purpose. Maddy let her keys clatter onto the counter, the noise breaking the tranquillity as she slumped into a chair by the table.

"Long day?" Her mother asked, glancing briefly over her shoulder before returning to her task. Her voice carried its usual mix of gentle concern and quiet insistence, the tone that had a way of coaxing the truth out of anyone who crossed her path.

"Understatement," Maddy said, swiping a slice of cucumber from the cutting board. "You wouldn't believe the things I've seen."

"Try me," Claire said, raising an eyebrow as she set the knife down.

Maddy hesitated, her fingers absently tracing the edge of the table. The weight of the case pressed hard against her chest, an invisible burden she couldn't quite share. She shook her head, forcing a smile that felt brittle. "Work stuff," she said finally. "You don't want to know. Really."

"You always do that," Claire said softly, her tone somewhere between reproach and concern. "Lock things away."

Maddy stared at the table, her throat tightening. "I'm just trying to keep you out of it, Mam."

Claire set down the knife and wiped her hands on a tea towel before resting them gently on Maddy's shoulder. Her touch was warm, grounding. "I'm already in it," she said softly. "You come home looking like this, like the world's on your shoulders, and it breaks my heart. I don't need the details to know it's bad. I just need to know you're okay."

Maddy managed a weak smile. "I'll figure it out."

"I know you will," Her mother gave her hand a small squeeze. "You always do."

* * *

Maddy's phone buzzed as she sat in her car the next morning, parked outside the station. Emily's name flashed across the screen.

"Maddy, you're gonna love me," Emily said the moment Maddy answered.

"You found our paramedic confessing on tape?" Maddy asked, sarcasm lacing her voice.

"Not quite, but close," Emily replied, her tone light but tinged with excitement. "I've been looking into his past postings. Guess who else had unexplained deaths while he was stationed there?"

Maddy straightened in her seat. "How many?"

"Three. And all had near-death experiences beforehand," Emily said, her words tumbling out.

Maddy's heart thudded. "Send me everything."

"You'll have it in two minutes," Emily said. "This guy's a bloody enigma, but you were right. The pattern's there."

* * *

Maddy stared at the files Emily had sent, her laptop screen glowing in the dim light of her office. Three more deaths, all tied to Daniel Cross, all as eerily unexplained as Sophie and Andy's. The pattern was undeniable, yet maddeningly elusive. No hard evidence, just threads of connection that felt as fragile as spider silk.

"This can't be a coincidence," Maddy whispered, her fingers tightening around her pen.

The photos of the victims stared back at her, their faces frozen in moments of peace that belied the chaos surrounding their deaths. He was involved, she could feel it in her gut, but proving it was another matter entirely.

Her phone buzzed again, pulling her out of her thoughts. Another text from the unknown number. This time, it read: *Stop while you have a chance.*

Maddy stared at the screen, ice flooding her veins. This wasn't vague anymore. This was a direct threat. Stop or else.

Chapter Five

"*Stop while you have a chance.*"

The words sat on Maddy's phone screen, taunting her with their simplicity. Her jaw tightened as she resisted the urge to throw the device across the room. Whoever was sending these messages clearly thought they were clever, thought they could rattle her. *Well, congratulations,* she thought bitterly. It was working.

Her finger hovered over the delete button before she stopped herself. No, she'd keep it. If this person thought they were intimidating her, they'd miscalculated. Instead, she saved the number under "Unknown Prick" and locked her phone, tossing it onto her cluttered desk with a loud clatter.

Maddy exhaled sharply and glanced at the mess around her. Case files, crime scene photos, and hastily scribbled notes were strewn across every available surface. Somewhere beneath the chaos was a cup of coffee that had gone cold hours ago. The thought of sorting through it all was overwhelming, but she knew the pressure in her chest wouldn't ease until she did.

. . .

"Good news!" Emily announced, bursting through into the communal offices with her usual whirlwind energy. She plonked a stack of folders on top of Maddy's already teetering pile with a grin. "I come bearing gifts."

Maddy raised an eyebrow. "If it's not chocolate, I'm not interested."

"Better than chocolate," Emily replied, flipping open the top file. "Daniel Cross' employment history. And let's just say it's full of red flags."

Maddy's pulse quickened as she reached for the folder. The sight of His name, typed neatly across the top of the page, sent a jolt through her. She thumbed through the papers, her brow furrowing as she read.

"He's moved around a lot," she said, pointing at the dates. "Every two or three years."

"Exactly," Emily said, pulling a chair closer and leaning over Maddy's shoulder. "And every time he leaves, there's a string of unexplained deaths that magically stop after he's gone."

Maddy tapped her pen against the desk, her mind racing as she scanned the pages. He'd worked in towns and cities all over the region, never staying in one place for too long. At each posting, there were clusters of deaths eerily similar to the ones in Whitby, people who'd survived near-death experiences, only to die under mysterious circumstances very shortly after.

"It's like he knows when to disappear," Maddy mumbled, more to herself than Emily.

"Or he plans it that way," Emily added grimly.

Maddy looked up to meet Emily's worried look. "If he's been doing this for years, why hasn't anyone noticed before?"

Emily shrugged. "Maybe no one was looking. Or maybe they didn't want to."

* * *

That night, Maddy found herself sitting at the kitchen table, her hands cradling a mug of tea Claire had made for her. The warmth seeped into her palms, grounding her for the first time all day.

"You look like you haven't slept in a week," Her mother sat herself down across from her. She studied Maddy with the sharp, assessing gaze that had once kept a classroom of teenagers in line.

"That's because I haven't," Maddy admitted, her voice flat.

Claire reached for the biscuit tin in the middle of the table and slid it toward her. "Have one. You'll feel better."

Maddy huffed a quiet laugh, taking a ginger biscuit and biting into it. "You know what's funny? You always think food solves everything."

"It doesn't hurt," Claire said with a shrug. She leaned forward, resting her elbows on the table. "But seriously, Maddy, you can't solve everything. Sometimes you need to step back."

Maddy shook her head, the weight of the case pressing hard against her chest. "Not this time, Mam. If I step back, someone might die."

Claire sighed, her expression softening. "You've always been like this. Even as a kid, you couldn't let things go. It's what makes you good at what you do, but it's also what's going to burn you out if you're not careful."

Maddy stared at the table, her throat tightening. "I just... I can't let him get away with it. Not this time."

Claire reached across the table, her hand covering Maddy's.

* * *

The next morning, Maddy was back at the station, poring over the files Emily had brought. Daniel Cross' employment history painted a damning picture, but it wasn't enough. She needed more, something concrete, something that couldn't be dismissed as coincidence.

"Maddy, you need to see this," Emily said, her voice urgent as she appeared in the doorway.

Maddy looked up from her notes, her brow furrowing. "What is it?"

Emily placed a printout on the desk and pointed to a series of timestamps. "Emergency response logs. Look at the times. Daniel was the first on scene for all three victims, and he arrived before the 999 calls were even logged."

Maddy's stomach dropped. "You're kidding."

Emily shook her head. "It's all here. He was already on site before dispatch even knew there was an emergency."

Maddy stared at the printout, her mind racing. *That was impossible. Unless...*

"He's picking them," Maddy whispered. "He's choosing who to save."

"And who not to," Emily added grimly.

The room seemed to close in around her as the implications sank in. Daniel wasn't just some unlucky paramedic caught in a string of coincidences, he was orchestrating them. Playing god. Deciding who lived and who didn't.

Chapter Six

The weight of the recent discoveries pressed against Maddy's chest, each new revelation stacking onto the last until it became impossible to ignore.

Emily sat across from her, her fingers skimming over her keyboard as she sifted through the growing mountain of evidence. "We need something solid," Maddy muttered, rubbing her temple. "Something that ties our paramedic to these deaths without a doubt."

Emily glanced up. "We're getting there. Look at this," she said, spinning the monitor towards Maddy. "Every town Daniel has worked in, there's a pattern. Each time he moves, there's a gap, a missing person. It's almost like clockwork."

Maddy leaned forward, scanning the names, dates, and locations Emily had pulled together. Her stomach twisted. Each location told a story, a town, a victim, and a paramedic who had arrived just in time. But never too early, and never too late. Always when fate had already twisted the knife. "If what we suspect is true, then we're not just looking at a serial killer," she said slowly. "We're looking at someone who's been refining his method for years, someone who's learned exactly how to make sure no one sees the pattern until it's too late."

Emily nodded. "And he's been getting away with it every time."

Maddy exhaled, her pulse kicking up a notch. "Not anymore."

***

Emily frowned at her screen. "Look at this. Gillian Longstaff, her husband, Peter, was one of the victims. She mentioned that Daniel Cross visited him two days before he died. That's... unusual, right?" She hesitated, clicking through the report again. "It wasn't just a casual visit either. He wasn't on duty. No emergency call was logged. He just showed up."

Maddy's stomach churned. "Not if he was checking on his work."

Emily's face darkened. "We need to talk to her."

The Longstaff house was a modest red-brick semi-detached property in the same style as the others on the street, its once-pristine garden now slightly overgrown, weeds creeping between the cracks of the pathway. The curtains were drawn despite the daylight, casting the house in a shadowed gloom. A faint scent of damp earth lingered in the air, carried by the breeze from the nearby fields. Maddy hesitated a beat before knocking on the door, the sharp sound cutting through the eerie silence of the quiet street. Somewhere in the distance a dog barked, but no other movement disturbed the stillness.

Gillian Longstaff opened the door hesitantly. She was in her mid-fifties, her face drawn, the weight of grief visible in the hollows beneath her eyes. "Detective?" she asked, her voice hoarse.

"Gillian, I know this is difficult. Thank you for accepting my call earlier, but we need to ask you a few questions about Peter," Maddy said, keeping her tone gentle. "May we come in?"

She hesitated before stepping back to usher them inside. The living room was slightly cluttered and the walls were lined with framed photographs, family snapshots, holiday pictures, moments frozen before everything changed.

Gillian perched on the edge of the sofa, clutching a tissue in her hands. "What do you need to know?"

Maddy took a seat opposite her. "You mentioned before that Daniel Cross, the paramedic who attended the scene, visited Peter a couple of days before he died. Can you tell us more about that?"

Gillian's fingers tightened around the tissue. "He came by unexpectedly. Said he just wanted to check in, see how Peter was recovering. I remember thinking how kind it was..." the woman's eyes went far away for a moment, "but..."

"But what?" Emily prompted gently.

Gillian hesitated, her gaze flickering to the mantelpiece where Peter's framed photograph sat. "He kept saying how lucky Peter was. Over and over. 'Not everyone gets a second chance,' he said. It unsettled me, in truth. At the time, I thought he meant it as encouragement, but now..." She trailed off, shaking her head.

Maddy's pulse pounded. "Did Peter mention anything about the visit afterwards? Did Daniel say anything else?"

Gillian swallowed hard. "Peter seemed uneasy. He said the paramedic asked a lot of questions. How he was feeling, if he'd been thinking about what happened. And then," she hesitated. "This might sound odd, but Peter said the man seemed almost disappointed. Like he expected him to say something different."

Emily and Maddy exchanged a look.

Maddy leaned forward. "Gillian, I need to ask, did Peter seem *afraid* of Daniel?"

Gillian hesitated for a moment, and the clock on the mantelpiece sliced a few more seconds off of their lives. Suddenly, she nodded. "Yes. Yes, I think he did."

* * *

As they stepped outside, Maddy scanned the street instinctively. A dark car sat parked further down, its windows tinted just enough to make it impossible to see inside. As soon as she and Emily moved towards their own car, the engine of the dark vehicle rumbled to life.

Maddy's stomach twisted as it slowly pulled away.

Emily exhaled sharply. "You saw that, right?"

Maddy nodded, her jaw tightening. "Yeah. I saw it."

They stood in silence for a beat, the hairs on Maddy's neck prickling.

* * *

The weight of it all pressed against Maddy's ribs as she sat in her dimly lit living room that night. Claire was in the kitchen, the clinking of cups against the counter, the only sign of life in the house.

"You look like hell," Claire commented, handing Maddy a mug of tea.

Maddy huffed a tired laugh. "Thanks, Mam. That's exactly what I needed to hear."

Claire sat across from her. "Long day?"

Maddy hesitated, staring into her cup. "Something like that."

Claire studied her. "You want to tell me what's eating at you?"

Maddy opened her mouth, then closed it. A thought lingered at the edges of her mind, a suspicion she couldn't quite put into words. It wasn't fully formed yet, just an inch beneath her skin, a sense that something wasn't adding up. She didn't know what it meant, not yet, but it wouldn't let her rest.

Instead, she shook her head. "It's just work." But the words felt hollow even as she said them. The unease gnawed at her, a whisper in the back of her mind that refused to be ignored. Something about this case, about Daniel Cross, about the way it all seemed too perfectly orchestrated, it wasn't just a killer's pattern. It was something else. Something personal. But until she could put her finger on it, all she could do was keep digging.

Claire didn't look convinced, but she let it go. "Just don't lose yourself in it, love."

*** * ***

Sleep didn't come easily for Maddy that night. When she finally gave up on trying, she found herself at the kitchen table, laptop open, fingers hovering over the keyboard.

She didn't want to look. Didn't want to dig into wounds that had barely healed. But that feeling, the gnawing suspicion that had been creeping through her mind all day, refused to let go. If she left it alone, she knew it would only fester, an unanswered question clawing at the back of her mind.

So, with a deep breath, she pushed aside the weight of hesitation and clicked the search bar.

Her breath hitched as she typed: **Frost, Jonathan. Police Officer. Fatal accident. Whitby.**

The report loaded, clinical and cold. It was dated three years ago. Her father's death, officially an accident. *Survived collision with vehicle at 35 mph. Minor injuries. Fatal accident three days later: hit-and-run, no suspect identified.*

Maddy's eyes skimmed lower in the article, and then froze.

Attending paramedic: Daniel Cross.

A sharp chill crawled down her spine. Her stomach turned to lead.

For a long moment she sat there, staring at the name. Disbelief warred with something darker, something more terrifying.

Had he been there that day? Had he looked into her father's eyes, knowing he wouldn't let him live?

Maddy's hands clenched into fists, nails digging into her palms. The room suddenly felt too small, the air too thick. The case had never been about her. She had told herself that from the start.

But now?

Now, she wasn't so sure.

Chapter Seven

The rain had started again, drumming steadily against the roof of Maddy's car, turning the windscreen into a canvas of shifting grey. The wipers worked in slow, rhythmic sweeps, but she barely registered the movement. Her fingers curled around the edges of the paper in her lap, her nails pressing half-moon indentations into the damp fibres. The words printed across the page seemed to shift, as her brain refused to process them properly.

Attending Paramedic: Daniel Cross.

She had read it at least twenty times already since she discovered it the previous night. Each time the impact felt the same; sharp and visceral, like something had been carved out of her chest.

Daniel Cross had been there. That night, when her father had been pulled from the wreck of his car, still alive. He had been the one to treat him. The one to stabilise him. The one who had, *supposedly*, saved him.

And then her father had died just three days later.

Just like Andy Pearson. Just like Sophie Chambers. Just like all the others.

Maddy exhaled sharply, pressing her forehead against the cool steering wheel. A bitter taste coated her tongue. All these years she had believed it had been a tragic accident. A twist of fate.

Fate had never played any role in it.

She knew she should be moving, heading to the station, but her body wouldn't cooperate. Her mind was caught in an endless loop, replaying the same thought...

Daniel Cross had been there.

He had been there the day of her father's accident.

A name that had meant nothing to her before was now a gaping wound, raw and open. Maddy knew it was ridiculous, but she blamed herself for not even noticing the paramedics name before. How could she not? Why hadn't she asked questions before?

He'd been at the scene. He'd seen her father walk away. And three days later, her father was dead.

She inhaled sharply, forcing the air into her lungs, her pulse hammering in her throat. She wanted to scream, to smash her fist against the dashboard, to do anything but sit there drowning in this newfound horror. But she couldn't afford to let herself lose control. Not now. Not with so much at stake.

Her father had been another name on a long list of tragedies, another thread in Daniel Cross' twisted belief system. That was what she needed to focus on. Not the personal pain, not the grief clawing at her insides. Just the facts. She had to prove it, prove that he was behind it all. Then, and only then, could she let herself feel.

With a sharp breath, she grabbed the printouts and shoved them into her bag. The rain continued to hammer down as she started the engine and pulled onto the road, feeling the weight of the past crowding around her every second.

* * *

By the time Maddy arrived at the station the tension in her body had only tightened, coiling around her spine like a vice. The world outside had felt too open, too exposed, but stepping inside the station didn't bring the relief she had hoped for. The air was thick with the scent of coffee and ink, and the usual morning buzz of ringing phones, rustling papers, and the murmur of officers. Conversations blurred together in a low hum, but Maddy barely heard them.

Emily, perched at her desk finishing off the last of her porridge pot, clocked her the moment she walked in. "God, you look like hell," she pointed out.

"You're not the first to tell me that recently," Maddy muttered, shrugging off her coat and dropping her bag onto her desk with a heavy thud. The hollow pang in her stomach reminded her she hadn't eaten breakfast. She had meant to grab something before leaving the house, but food had been the last thing on her mind.

Emily frowned, setting her spoon down and folding her arms. "I mean it, Mads. You haven't slept, have you?"

Maddy flicked open her laptop, eyes scanning the screen though the words blurred. "I'll sleep when I have him in cuffs."

Emily wheeled her chair closer, lowering her voice. "This about what you found last night?" She hesitated. "Sorry, I didn't get a chance to reply to your message about finding something..."

Maddy didn't answer. Couldn't. The words were lodged somewhere in her throat, too raw to push out. She wasn't ready to say it aloud, to make it real. Not yet.

Instead, she shook her head, standing abruptly. "I need to talk to Harper."

***

Harper wasn't thrilled to see her storm into his office, files in hand and determination set into every line of her face. The space was as cluttered as ever, piles of paperwork threatening to collapse, an old coffee cup balanced precariously near the edge of his desk. He rubbed at his temples before sighing, clearly bracing for a fight.

"Maddy, I have a feeling I know what this is about, and I'm already exhausted," he grumbled, checking the time on his watch as if hoping she'd take the hint and leave.

"Then you'd better get some coffee, sir," she replied, unbothered, "because we need to talk."

She dropped the file onto his desk with a firm thud. "I've traced Daniel Cross to at least six locations where unexplained deaths have followed near-death incidents. He moves, people die, he moves again. It's a pattern. A very clear one."

Harper leaned back, exhaling through his nose. "You're stretching, Frost. I'm not saying I don't see the links, but it's circumstantial. He's a fucking paramedic. Of course he's been at the scene of emergencies."

Maddy's jaw clenched. "Coincidence doesn't kill people, sir. Men like Daniel do."

Harper rubbed a hand down his face, exhaling sharply. "What do you want, Frost? A full investigation? You don't have enough to get a warrant, let alone a conviction."

Maddy didn't sit. She planted her hands on the desk, leaning in, her voice unwavering. "Then we build a case, sir. We dig until we have enough to take to the CPS. But ignoring this? That's not an option."

Harper let out a dry chuckle, shaking his head. "You think I don't want to nail him if he's dirty? But I have to work with evidence, not just gut feelings. And right now, all you've got is a hunch and a few deaths that don't add up."

Maddy tapped the open file in front of him, forcing him to look at the neatly documented timeline of deaths. "It's more than a hunch. Six locations, sir. Six unexplained deaths following near-fatal accidents. The one common factor? Cross. That's not coincidence. That's a pattern."

Harper eyed her carefully, his fingers steepled in front of him. His gaze was unreadable, but she knew him well enough to recognise when he was weighing his options. "A pattern isn't proof. You know that."

She clenched her fists at her sides, frustration brimming. "He arrived at some scenes before the 999 calls are even logged, sir. Emergency response records show he was already on-site before dispatch knew there was an emergency. How does a paramedic just happen to be there before anyone calls for help?"

Harper's expression shifted slightly. She'd landed a blow.

"That's not coincidence," she pressed. "That's premeditation."

"Then let's get proof. Let's talk to the people he worked with, the families of the victims. Someone, somewhere, has seen something. We just have to find it."

Maddy glared at her superior. He *had* to give her this. Every murderer left something behind, something out of place...there was always a clue. You cannot just rip someone from the fabric of their life like that without leaving a frayed thread....

And all I have to do is find those threads and pull on them. That's all. Just give me that chance, Maddy silently prayed.

Silence stretched between them. The fluorescent light above flickered once, buzzing faintly as if filling the space where words should be. Harper exhaled slowly, rubbing his temples again like he already regretted where this conversation was heading.

"You really aren't going to let this go, are you?" he said.

Maddy met his gaze head-on, unwavering. "Not a chance."

* * *

Emily wheeled her chair closer to Maddy's desk. "Okay, if we're doing this, we need to be smart. Let's start with his paramedic records."

They spent hours combing through databases, pulling old paramedic reports, tracing Daniel's movements over the years. The deeper they dug, the more inconsistencies emerged. Gaps in his transfers, missing files, cases that should have been routine but had unusual endings. Every time he moved, unexplained fatalities followed.

Maddy rubbed at her temples, exhaustion creeping into her bones. "This isn't just coincidence. Look at this one, cardiac arrest, no pre-existing conditions. He was first on the scene."

Emily frowned. "And here, trauma victim, stable at hospital, suddenly deteriorates. Daniel Cross was the last one in the room before the decline."

Maddy leaned closer, flipping through another set of reports. "And this one, respiratory failure post-surgery, patient had been improving until guess who was present during rounds. It's too clean, Emily. Too perfect."

Emily sat back in her chair, stretching her arms above her head. "This is bloody ridiculous," she muttered. "How has no one noticed this before?"

Maddy ran a hand through her hair, exhaling sharply. "Because no one was looking for it. He knows how to blend in, how to make sure nothing ever points directly at him. If we hadn't started digging, we'd never have seen the pattern either."

Emily scrolled through another page of reports, shaking her head. "It's not just luck. It's control. He's not just a first responder, he's positioning himself where he wants to be. He's..." she hesitated, staring at the screen. "He's playing God."

Maddy swallowed hard, staring at the evidence stacking up in front of them. The thought had been lingering at the edges of her mind, but hearing Emily say it out loud made it real. "And we have to stop him before he does it again."

* * *

By the time Maddy returned to her mother's cottage, it was late afternoon and exhaustion pressed heavy against her shoulders, but she pushed it aside. The street was still empty, the rain easing into a fine mist. The familiar warmth of home should have been comforting, but as she reached for her keys, something caught her eye.

A small, white envelope, resting on her doorstep.

A chill crawled up her spine as she bent down, fingers trembling slightly as she picked it up. The paper was damp, curling at the edges. No address, no name. Just two words, scrawled in smudged ink:

Let it go.

Her breath hitched. The cold settled deep in her bones.

Instead of fear, something else burned in her chest. Anger. Resolve.

The rain started again, heavier this time, but she didn't move from where she stood. The note crumpled in her grip, but her expression remained unreadable.

She stared at it for a long moment, then pulled out her phone and dialled.

"We need to move on it. Now."

Chapter Eight

Maddy gripped the steering wheel, her fingers flexing before tightening again. She could still feel the phantom sensation of the note in her palm, the weight of it heavier than mere paper. Someone had walked up to her mother's cottage, placed it on the step, and left. They'd known where she lived. Where *her mother* lived.

The idea sent a slow coil of anger twisting through her stomach.

She should tell Harper. Or at least Emily. But she could already hear what they'd say. *Step back, Maddy. Take a breath. This is getting too close.*

Too close? The thought almost made her laugh. It had *always* been close. She just hadn't realised that until now.

Instead, she shoved the note into the glove compartment and started the engine. If whoever left it thought she'd scare easily, then they didn't know her at all.

* * *

Emily was waiting at her desk when Maddy walked into the station, a takeaway coffee in her hand. "You look like you slept in a crime scene."

Maddy dropped into her chair, rubbing at the tension in her neck. "Feel like it too."

Emily slid the coffee across the desk. "This might help."

Maddy took it, grateful. "Tell me you've got something."

Emily tapped at her laptop, bringing up a profile. "Ellie Rogers. Former nurse, worked with Daniel Cross at two different hospitals before he came to Whitby. She left suddenly, no explanation. Now she's renting a small place just outside town."

Maddy straightened. This could be it. This could be the break they've been waiting for. "Think she saw something?"

Emily hesitated. "I think she *knows* something."

Maddy drained half the coffee in one gulp and stood. "Then let's go."

* * *

The drive was quiet, the tension inside the car thick as the North Sea mist rolling in from the coast. The roads were slick from last night's rain, puddles forming in the dips where the tarmac had cracked.

Emily glanced at Maddy as she turned onto the main road. "You're acting like this is personal."

Maddy's hands tightened on the wheel. "Because it is."

Emily exhaled through her nose but didn't argue. Instead, she pulled up Ellie's information on her phone. "She left her last job abruptly. No complaints filed against her, no record of misconduct. Just...gone."

Maddy nodded. It fit the pattern. People who got too close to him had a habit of disappearing one way or another.

They turned onto a narrow lane, the houses sparse, most with overgrown hedgerows and driveways filled with battered cars. It was a typical run-down, edge-of-town sink neighbourhood. A place where quiet people struggled for the remnants of a life, after society had chewed them up and spat them back out again. Ellie's place was a small bungalow, the curtains drawn despite the early-ish hour.

Maddy killed the engine. "Let's see what she has to say."

Ellie answered on the third knock. She was in her early forties, brown hair pulled back into a loose bun. Her eyes flickered between them, cautious, as if already preparing to shut the door in their faces.

Maddy flashed her badge. "Ellie Rogers? DS Frost. This is DC Ward. We have just a few questions to ask."

The woman hesitated, then stepped back, allowing them inside.

The house was sparsely furnished, the kind of place that suggested she wasn't planning to stay long. A half-packed suitcase sat in the corner.

Emily shot Maddy a look but didn't say anything.

Ellie folded her arms. "I don't know what this is about."

Maddy didn't move from where she stood. "Daniel Cross."

The reaction was immediate. Ellie's jaw tensed, her shoulders stiffening like she'd been braced for the name but still hadn't wanted to hear it.

"I don't-"

Maddy cut her off. "You worked with him. Twice. And both times, you left without notice."

Ellie exhaled through her nose. "I don't know anything."

Maddy took a step closer. "You do."

The woman's eyes darted past her, like she was checking the windows. Checking for someone else. "Some things are better left buried," the nurse said in a quiet voice.

Maddy ignored the chill that crept up her spine. "Not if people are dying because of them."

Ellie swallowed. Her hands trembled slightly as she reached for the armrest of the chair beside her. "He always knew," she murmured.

Maddy frowned. "Knew what?"

Ellie's gaze flicked to her, something haunted in her expression. "When it was their time."

Silence settled heavily between them. The detectives exchanged a glance, mutually recognising that this was confirmation of what they feared.

Emily was the first to break it. "You need to tell us everything."

But Ellie shook her head. "I...I can't."

Maddy opened her mouth to push further, but Ellie was already moving, walking toward the door. "I think we're done here."

Maddy ground her teeth. so much more she wanted to ask. Wanted to know, but instead nodded. "If you remember anything else..."

Ellie didn't look back as she opened the door. "I won't."

* * *

As they walked back to the car, Maddy's gut twisted. They had something. Not much, but something. Daniel Cross wasn't just a paramedic with a suspicious number of deaths trailing behind him. He was watching. Waiting.

Choosing.

She opened the driver's door, but something made her pause. A prickle at the back of her neck.

She turned her head slightly, catching sight of a dark car parked a few houses down. The windows were tinted, and the engine was running. The moment she moved, it pulled away, tyres crunching over wet gravel.

Maddy watched it disappear around the corner.

"They weren't just warning her any more," she murmured. "They were watching."

* * *

Later that night, Maddy sat at her kitchen table, files spread in front of her, but she couldn't focus.

She kept thinking about Ellie. About the way her voice had wavered. The way she had looked over Maddy's shoulder, as if expecting Daniel Cross to be standing right there.

Her phone buzzed.

Emily: *We need to move faster.*

Maddy stared at the screen for a long moment before typing back: *Tomorrow. First thing.*

She locked the phone and exhaled. He wasn't just a name on a file any more.

He was a shadow in her rearview mirror.

And she wasn't about to let him stay there.

Chapter Nine

The morning air was crisp, biting at Maddy's skin as she stepped outside, with the dampness of last night's rain still clinging to the streets. Whitby always had a certain eerie charm in the early hours, when the mist from the North Sea rolled through the town, seeping into every narrow alleyway and curling around the old, weathered buildings. Normally, she found it oddly comforting. Today, it set her teeth on edge.

She double-checked the lock on the cottage door, then checked it again. Claire was still asleep inside, oblivious to the threat that hung over all of them. Maddy should have told her about the note. About finding it on the doorstep. About all of it. But what good would that have done? All it would achieve was worry, and Claire had already lost enough in her life, hadn't she?

Her boots crunched against the gravel as she made her way to the car, but she paused before getting in, scanning the quiet street. The usual parked cars, the same houses with their drawn curtains and empty driveways. It should have felt normal.

It didn't.

As she drove, she kept checking her mirrors, slowing a little more than usual at every turn and junction to make sure. And then she saw it. A dark car, maybe black or navy, it was hard to tell in the grey morning light, sitting two cars back. It wasn't following too closely, but it stayed with her through three turns, never overtaking, never slowing enough to let more than two vehicles slip between them.

Her pulse thudded in her ears. She made an abrupt left onto a side street, a longer way to the station, but one with fewer exits. If they turned in after her...

The car glided past the junction without hesitation, continuing straight as if she'd never been there.

Maddy exhaled, her grip on the wheel loosening, but the tension in her gut remained. They weren't just warning her any more. They wanted her to feel it.

Emily was already at her desk when Maddy strode into the station, her fingers flying across her keyboard, eyes locked onto the screen. She barely glanced up when Maddy dropped into her chair, but when she did, her brow furrowed.

"You alright?"

"Close enough," Maddy muttered, rubbing at her temples. "What have you got?"

Emily spun her monitor towards Maddy. "Cross' employment history. Something's off."

Maddy leaned in, scanning the highlighted sections. Hospital transfers, ambulance services in different towns. None of it was unusual on its own, but together..?

Her stomach tightened as she followed Emily's cursor across the screen. Every two to three years, he moved on. Never staying long enough to build deep roots, but just enough to leave a trail. Not a blatant one. A carefully concealed, almost surgical pattern of silence and erasure.

He never stays anywhere more than two, three years at most," Emily pointed out, scrolling further. "And every time he moves, there's a spike in unexplained deaths. Not just in hospitals either, some in private care, some outside medical settings entirely. It's like wherever he is, people just... expire."

Maddy's stomach turned. She scanned through the records, her mind racing. "Any complaints? Investigations? Anything that could explain why he left?"

Emily shook her head, clicking through different reports. "Nothing. Not one single complaint against him. Not one inquiry. It's like he was never there." She leaned back in her chair, rubbing at her temple. "I don't get it. No one works in emergency care that long without someone filing a grievance. A bad call. A mistake. Something."

Maddy felt a cold weight settle in her gut. She agreed. It was the same with all of the services, as far as she was aware. You couldn't work in these jobs, dealing with people on their very worst days, with snap decisions being made and emotions at an all-time high without someone deciding to file a complaint. Sometimes they had actual grievances, and sometimes it was because the victim just couldn't understand what had just happened to them, or why.

Maddy tapped her hand on the desk. "Unless someone made sure those questions were never asked."

Emily glanced up sharply. "Exactly. And look at this." She pulled up another file. "Every transfer was processed normally. Different HR departments, different hospitals, different trusts. No one person overseeing it all."

Maddy leaned closer, scanning the documents. "So each

place only saw their own clean record. No complaints filed, positive references from colleagues, saves lives on the job. Why would they question a transfer request?"

"They wouldn't," Emily said. "And with the NHS being what it is, staff moving around is common. Paramedics transfer all the time for personal reasons, career progression, closer to family. It's not suspicious."

"Especially if he's careful about timing," Maddy added. "Moves before anyone connects the dots. Before the deaths stack up enough to raise flags. By the time someone might notice a pattern, he's already gone and it's the next trust's problem."

Emily scrolled through the timeline. "And he never stays long enough for anyone to look too closely. Two years here, three years there. Just a dedicated paramedic moving on. Each new employer sees a spotless record and never thinks to dig deeper."

"Because why would they?" Maddy said bitterly. "He's not leaving problems behind. Just unexplained deaths that get chalked up to natural causes or delayed trauma. Nothing that points back to him."

The realisation made Maddy's skin prickle. Daniel hadn't just been lucky. Had someone else been looking out for him, clearing the path, ensuring his record remained spotless? Someone higher up than even he was, with the ability to clear hospital records across multiple sites?

Her tapping turned into a drumbeat, her mind already jumping ahead. "We need to find out who signed off on his transfers. Who kept his record clean."

Emily was already ahead of her, fingers moving across the keyboard. "On it."

Before she could pull up the next file, DC Ben Travers appeared at Emily's desk, slightly out of breath.

"Ward, you were going to follow up with that nurse, weren't you? Ellie Rogers?"

Emily looked up. "Yeah, why?"

"Just had a call come through from the front desk. Her neighbour's downstairs reporting her missing. Apparently Ellie was supposed to meet her for coffee yesterday evening. Some regular thing they do, and never showed. Neighbour went round this morning, no answer, car's still there but the house is locked up tight."

Maddy's head snapped up. "When did the neighbour last see her?"

Travers checked his notes. "Day before yesterday. Said Ellie seemed jumpy after the police visited, mentioned something about needing to leave town."

Emily and Maddy exchanged a look.

"The neighbour also mentioned a car," Travers continued. "Sat idling outside Ellie's place for ages the night you visited. Engine running, just sitting there. She thought it was odd but didn't think much of it at the time."

Maddy's stomach dropped. "He got to her."

"Or she bolted," Emily said quietly, though her expression suggested she didn't believe it.

Travers shifted uncomfortably. "You want to take the report, or should I pass it to someone else?"

"We'll take it," Maddy said immediately. "Get her details out to all stations. Hospitals, transport hubs, everything."

Travers nodded and headed back downstairs.

Maddy exhaled through her nose, steeling herself. If no one had asked the questions before, they damn well would now.

* * *

Dr. Patel was waiting in the morgue when Maddy arrived, his usual detached expression in place. But his hands, resting on the steel table, were tighter than usual. His usual air of methodical calm was still there, but something about the way he carried himself today was different. There was tension in his shoulders, something lurking behind his sharp gaze that made Maddy's stomach tighten.

"You're going to want to see this," the coroner said, leading her past rows of cold storage drawers toward his desk, where printouts were spread in careful disorder.

Maddy scanned the toxicology reports, her fingers trailing over the pages. Elevated adrenaline. Spiked cortisol. Abnormal neural activity. A pattern repeating itself across multiple victims.

"This was Sophie Chambers?" she asked.

"And Andy Pearson," Patel added, flipping another report over to show identical readings. "And another case from Daniel's previous station, one that hadn't raised any red flags, until now."

Maddy's throat tightened. The results and graphs meant nothing to her. "And what exactly does this tell us?"

Patel let out a slow breath, his eyes lingering on the data as if he was still trying to convince himself of the conclusion. "It's like they saw something," he murmured. "Like they knew what was coming. And their bodies reacted before they even had the chance to fight."

Maddy's skin prickled. "Fight what?"

Patel hesitated. His fingers tapped once against the desk, a rare tell that gave away his unease. "Fear triggers a physiological response, we know that," he said. "A burst of adrenaline, heightened awareness. But these levels," He pointed at the readings. "These aren't normal. They're excessive. Off the charts. This isn't just fight-or-flight. It's like their bodies were in a full-scale panic before they died."

Maddy swallowed, her pulse quickening. "Which means what exactly, Patel? That they saw something? That someone made sure they felt panic before they died?"

Patel's lips pressed into a thin line. "I can't tell you how, but I can tell you this, these people didn't just pass away peacefully. Something triggered this. Their nervous systems went into overdrive and full system shock, causing their hearts to stop."

Maddy clenched her jaw. "You're saying Daniel Cross didn't just kill them. He made them...what, experience their worst fears?"

Dr. Patel shook his head in frustration or disgust. He didn't answer immediately, which was worse than anything he could have said. When he finally spoke, his voice was quieter than before, like he didn't want the words to be real. "I can't say what they saw or experienced, unfortunately. But what is the most terrifying experience for all of us? I would say our own death."

Maddy exhaled sharply, gripping the edge of the table as her mind reeled. He wasn't just choosing his victims, he was doing something to them before they died. Making them know it was coming. Making them feel it so viscerally, that their hearts stopped.

A slow, icy dread curled around her spine. She had spent so much time trying to prove he was responsible for these deaths, trying to connect him to them. But this? This was something else entirely. This wasn't just murder.

It was cruelty.

* * *

Back at the station, Maddy stormed past the desks, barely registering Emily's concerned glance as she made a beeline for

Harper's office. Her heart was still pounding from Patel's revelation. If she didn't push now, if she didn't get ahead of this, Daniel would slip away again.

The man who killed my father will walk free. And do it all again...

She wasn't letting that happen. Not this time.

She didn't bother knocking. The door swung open with a forceful push, drawing Harper's immediate scowl as he looked up from a stack of reports.

"Frost," he said, setting his pen down. "Sit."

She dropped into the chair across from his desk, arms folded, shoulders locked tight. "Sir, we need to take this to the next level. I've got Patel's analysis, and..."

Harper exhaled through his nose. "No."

She blinked. "No?"

"You need to step back."

Her jaw clenched, heat rising in her chest. "We have evidence,"

Harper held up a hand. "You have a theory," he said flatly. "A strong one, I'll give you that. But you're too close to this. You're making mistakes."

Maddy inhaled sharply, forcing herself to stay calm. "Sir, Daniel Cross has been linked to multiple suspicious deaths. We've traced his movements, we've got forensic anomalies, we-"

"Have nothing a CPS lawyer wouldn't laugh out of court," Harper interrupted, his voice sharp but not unkind. "Adrenaline spikes? A pattern of locations? You think that's going to stand up in front of a jury?" He leaned back in his chair, eyes pinning her in place. "We need something solid, Frost. Something undeniable."

She could feel her pulse hammering in her temples. "So, what? We sit on our hands? Wait for him to do it again?"

Harper's lips pressed into a thin line. "I have to work within the law, and right now, all you've got is a hunch wrapped in circumstantial evidence."

Maddy's hands curled into fists on her lap. "Six victims, sir. Six unexplained deaths, all after near-fatal incidents. And Daniel? He was there. Every single time."

Harper sighed, rubbing his temples. "And what if you're wrong, Frost?" he asked quietly. "What if this is nothing more than bad luck and coincidence?"

She stared at him, disbelief curling in her gut. "Then I'll admit I was wrong. But if I'm right? If I step back, and he kills someone else?" Her voice dropped, quiet but firm. "That's on me. And I can't live with that."

Harper studied her for a long moment, his fingers steepled in front of him. Then, finally, he sighed. "Look, I know this case is important to you. I know you want justice. But you're walking a thin line, Frost. You keep pushing like this, and you won't like where it ends."

Maddy knew this dance well enough. Harper had always managed his team the same way: give them rope, watch how they used it. Push too far, and he'd pull you back hard. Stay just inside the lines, and he'll give you room to work. It was how he'd mentored her years ago, and clearly, nothing had changed.

A cold prickle ran down her spine, but she didn't back down. "Noted," she said, standing.

Harper didn't stop her as she walked out. But his words followed her, heavy and suffocating.

And she had a feeling she knew exactly what he meant.

* * *

The note was waiting for her when she left the station, tucked neatly under her windscreen wiper.

You should have listened.

She stared at it, the ink slightly smudged from the damp air. Her skin prickled as she scanned the street. No dark car. No watching eyes.

But they were there. She knew it.

The warning had changed.

It wasn't a suggestion any more.

It was a promise.

Chapter Ten

Maddy sat in her car outside the office of Tom Denton, former investigative journalist turned freelance. She had debated whether this was a mistake all morning, but the alternative, doing nothing, was worse. If she was going to take Daniel Cross down, she needed someone who wasn't bound by police red tape. Someone like Tom.

Tom Denton had always had a knack for getting under her skin. He had once been a respected name in crime reporting before his stubbornness and disregard for authority burned too many bridges. He wasn't afraid to ask the questions no one else would, and to dig where others wouldn't dare. That made him reckless, but it also made him exactly who she needed right now.

Their history was complicated. Years ago, when she was still adjusting to life as a detective, they had been something, whatever that meant. A tangle of late-night conversations, unresolved tension, and the kind of chemistry that should've led somewhere but never quite did. His obsession with chasing the truth had always come first, and her job didn't allow for distractions. They had parted ways, though neither had ever quite let go of the frustration, the 'almosts' that still lingered between them.

She grabbed her coat and stepped out, pulling the collar up against the sharp Whitby wind. The old office building loomed above her, faded signage barely legible from years of exposure to the salt air. This shabby and slow decay suited Tom just fine, as had never cared for appearances.

Maddy paused outside knowing she shouldn't be there. Every instinct told her this was bending protocol, but Tom had access she needed. If she walked away now, she would lose the thread. She tightened her jaw, knowing she would face Harper's anger later, but knocked on the door anyway.

When it opened, Tom's familiar smirk greeted her, but there was wariness behind his eyes.

"Mads, I should've known you wouldn't just come by for a friendly chat. What have you got for me?"

Inside, the office smelled of stale coffee and ink, cluttered with notebooks, old case files, and a half-eaten sandwich left abandoned on his desk. Maddy hovered near the door for a moment, taking in the familiar chaos. It hadn't changed much, not that she'd expected it to. Tom had always been like this. Brilliant, infuriatingly stubborn, and completely incapable of keeping an organised workspace.

He caught her glance and smirked. "Still judging my filing system?"

She snorted, shrugging off her coat and draping it over the nearest chair. "Filing system? That's generous. This place looks like a crime scene."

"Journalism isn't tidy," he said, leaning against his desk. "Mess is where the truth is. But I'm guessing you didn't come here to critique my office."

Maddy hesitated, shifting her weight. Now that she was

here, sitting face to face with him again after all this time, it felt...strange. Unfinished.

Tom leaned forward, watching her with that sharp, knowing gaze. "Go on, then. Tell me why you're really here."

She exhaled and pulled out the file, laying it down between them. "It's about Daniel Cross."

His smirk faded, replaced by interest. "The paramedic?"

"Not just a paramedic. A killer." She tapped the pages, pointing at highlighted sections. "There's a pattern, he moves to a new area, people survive close calls, and then they die under mysterious circumstances days later. No clear cause. No obvious foul play. Just...gone."

Tom picked up the file and skimmed through it, his brow furrowing. "And you think he's doing this on purpose?"

"I know he is."

He exhaled, setting the papers down. "Jesus, Maddy. This is...this is one hell of an accusation."

"I wouldn't be here if I didn't have something," she said, leaning in. "And it's not just the deaths. It's what happened after we spoke to the witnesses. Ellie Rogers, the nurse who worked with him, was terrified when we interviewed her. Told us Daniel always knew when it was someone's time. A bit later, she vanished. House locked up, car still in the driveway, but she's gone. No word. No trace."

Tom ran a hand through his hair, his usual cocky confidence replaced by something more serious. "You realise what you're saying, right? You're chasing a story that no one else has even whispered about. That means you're either onto something huge, or you're about to get yourself buried."

Maddy swallowed hard. She thought of the little, perfect white envelope, sitting on her mam's front step. "I'm already in too deep to stop now."

For a moment, neither of them spoke. The rain drummed

against the window, filling the silence between them. Then, Tom sat back, folding his arms. "Alright. I'll dig into his background, see what I can find. But you need to be careful, Mads. If this guy is as bad as you think, stirring the pot could make you a target."

She met his gaze, her jaw set. "He already knows I'm looking."

* * *

Back at the station, Emily intercepted Maddy before she reached her desk, her expression already dark with frustration. "You talked to Tom," she accused, her arms folded so tightly across her chest it looked like she was holding herself back from shaking Maddy by the shoulders. "He's already been ringing round asking questions. Called here asking about Cross' shift patterns. Harper's going to flip when he finds out."

Maddy sighed, setting her bag down with more force than necessary. Exhaustion gnawed at her, but she squared her shoulders. "I need someone who's willing to go where we can't, Emily. You don't have to like it, but you know I'm right."

Emily's nostrils flared. "That's not how this works, Maddy! You can't just bring a journalist into an active investigation like he's some bloody extension of the team."

Maddy scoffed. "And what do you want me to do? Sit on my hands while Daniel keeps stacking bodies?"

Emily stepped closer, lowering her voice. "I want you to stop acting like you're the only one who cares about this."

Maddy's jaw clenched. "Then help me. Because we're running out of time, Emily. Every day we sit on this, Daniel is out there picking his next victim."

Emily shook her head, her face tight with disappointment.

"I want to trust you, but you're making that really bloody difficult."

The younger officer turned and walked away, her footsteps heavy against the station floor. Maddy stood there, surrounded by the hum of the busy station, but feeling more alone than ever.

Maddy was still at her desk, exhaustion clawing at her as she combed through the latest batch of reports, searching for anything they might have missed. She rubbed at her temple, the dull throb of an oncoming headache making itself known. She needed rest, proper rest, but that wasn't happening any time soon. Not with everything closing in.

She sighed, shutting her laptop and gathering her things. The day had been long, filled with dead ends and Harper's warning still ringing in her ears. She was halfway to the door when her phone buzzed in her pocket. She pulled it out, expecting another message from Emily, but instead, Tom's name flashed on the screen.

Meet me at The Blue Anchor. Found something.

Maddy frowned, her pulse kicking up. Tom wasn't generally a chatty man. He wasn't the sort to send messages like that unless he had something worth sharing. She hesitated for only a second before pushing through the station doors and heading straight for her car.

Emily's earlier words still echoed in her mind. Was she being reckless? Probably. But she'd made her choice the moment she decided to involve Tom.

The night air was thick with moisture as she walked into the pub. The low murmur of conversation, the clink of glasses, and the faint scent of stale beer gave the place its usual warmth, but something about it felt off. A prickle of unease crept up her spine. She scanned the room quickly. Tom wasn't there.

She approached the bar, leaning against the counter, her pulse hammering against her ribs. The bartender, a wiry man with deep lines etched into his face, eyed her curiously, pausing for only a moment before reaching under the counter. He slid a napkin across to her, his fingers hesitant, as if he didn't want to be the one delivering the message.

Maddy frowned, flipping it over. Three words, written in a shaky hand: *Too late, Madeline.*

Her stomach lurched. The noise of the pub faded into static. The hairs on the back of her neck rose. She forced herself to keep her breathing as she looked up at the bartender.

"Who gave you this?"

The man swallowed, his throat bobbing. "Some bloke. Didn't stay. Just said you'd know what it meant."

A cold weight settled in her chest. She pushed off from the counter, shoving the napkin into her pocket as she turned towards the door, every nerve in her body screaming that she was running out of time.

Her stomach clenched. The air in the room felt suddenly too thick, the familiar pub now an unfamiliar threat. She spun on her heel, shoving past a group of drinkers, her heart still racing as she bolted for the door.

* * *

Maddy skidded into the alley behind the pub, breath catching when she saw him, Tom slumped against the wall, blood trickling from a gash above his eye. His shirt was rumpled, his hands weakly gripping at the damp pavement as if he had been trying to steady himself.

She crouched beside him, heart pounding. "Tom? Tom, can you hear me?"

His head lolled slightly, a grimace tugging at his lips. "You," he rasped, coughing. "You took your time."

She reached out, pressing her fingers lightly against his chin, turning his face towards her so she could get a better look at his injury. The gash was deep but not life-threatening. Blood was already clotting around the edges.

"What the hell happened?" she asked, voice sharp, barely disguising the panic beneath it.

Tom coughed again, wincing. "Guess I got too close to the truth."

His breath hitched as he tried to sit up, and Maddy caught his arm, steadying him. He waved her off. "Someone was waiting for me. Jumped me before I even got in the pub."

Maddy's stomach twisted. "Did you see who?"

Tom exhaled shakily, pressing his hand to his ribs. "No. Just a shadow. But they had a message for me."

She swallowed. "What message?"

His fingers twitched, barely able to form a fist. "Drop the story." His voice was hoarse, barely more than a whisper. "And then, just before I blacked out...they said your name."

Maddy's breath stilled in her throat.

"This wasn't just about silencing you," she murmured, voice cold. "It was about sending a message to me."

* * *

As Maddy watched the nurse take Tom through into the A&E triage room, her hands curled into fists. The sterile brightness of the hospital entrance clashed with the darkness pooling in her chest, a storm she could barely contain. Her pulse thrummed in her ears, a deafening reminder of how close this had come to something much worse.

He could have died. Because of me!

She exhaled sharply, rubbing a hand over her face, the dampness of the rain clinging to her skin, mixing with the heat of her anger.

The journey here had been a blur, a mix of Tom's laboured breathing, the metallic tang of blood in the air, and her own silent fury. She had driven fast, her knuckles white on the wheel, barely stopping at lights, ignoring the occasional glance Tom had thrown her way. Now, standing there, she could feel the weight of it all pressing down. Every missed opportunity, every step too slow, every moment she had thought she was ahead only to find she had been playing into Daniel's hands all along.

Her fists clenched tighter. He wanted her rattled. He wanted her to back down.

Not a chance.

Maddy turned on her heel and strode towards her car, each step more determined than the last. He had made his move. Now, it was her turn.

Chapter Eleven

Maddy sat at her desk, rubbing at her temples as she tried to push back the ache that had settled behind her eyes. The only light in the station came from the harsh glow of her monitor and the dull flicker of the streetlamp outside, filtering through the window. Rain pattered softly against the glass, blurring the world beyond.

Her desk was a mess of paper, case files, old post-mortems, hastily written notes in red ink that formed an erratic map of connections only she could decipher. She leaned forward, scanning the documents with a weary focus. The exhaustion clung to her like a second skin, her muscles stiff from hours of sitting, but she refused to stop. Not now. Not when she was close.

Her body was screaming for rest. She could feel it in the way her hands trembled slightly when she reached for her pen, the way her eyes burned from staring at the screen for too long. But her mind wouldn't let go. She'd rest when Daniel Cross was behind bars.

A faint creak signalled Emily's arrival before she spoke. "Still going, then?"

Maddy didn't look up. "Still breathing, aren't I?"

Emily sighed, stepping fully into the room. She had two steaming mugs in her hands and placed one on Maddy's desk. "You look like a ghost. Drink that before you pass out."

Maddy muttered a thanks, wrapping her fingers around the porcelain, letting the warmth seep into her chilled skin.

Emily pulled up a chair and peered at the files strewn across the desk. "We're missing something."

"We're missing a lot of things," Maddy replied, pushing a paper aside to make room for the tea. "But we've got enough to start pulling threads."

They worked in silence for a while, the only sound the scratch of a pen against paper and the quiet hum of the station. They pinned crime scene photos and locations to a cork-board, drawing lines between Daniel's postings, the victims, and the deaths that followed.

Emily exhaled sharply. "Why is he so bloody careful? No CCTV, no direct evidence, no reports that ever got flagged. It's like he's a ghost."

Maddy tapped her pen against the board, frowning. "Not a ghost. A predator. And predators follow patterns."

For the first time, doubt crept into her thoughts. Was she chasing a phantom? Was this just a series of coincidences, or had Cross been slipping through the cracks for years? She flexed her fingers, the frustration coiling tight in her chest.

Emily nudged her foot under the table. "Hey. You're not losing it, okay? We *are* right. We just have to prove it."

Maddy forced a tight smile but said nothing.

By the time Emily stretched and let out a yawn, the station was eerily quiet, the usual bustle of officers long gone. "Right," the detective constable said, standing. "I need actual sleep, and you need to go home before you keel over."

Maddy scoffed. "Not likely."

They made their way through the station, their footsteps echoing in the near-empty corridors. Most of the desks were vacant now, the evening shift having wound down. A few stragglers remained, PC Phillips typing up a last-minute report, Sergeant Harris sipping coffee as he leaned against the reception desk, chatting with one of the newer recruits. Maddy nodded at them as she passed, offering a tired but acknowledging glance. The station air was thick with the smell of stale coffee and printer ink, but outside, the cool night air hit her skin like a slap. It should have been refreshing. Instead, it sent a chill down her spine.

Her steps slowed. Across the road, barely visible under the weak glow of the street-light, a dark car sat idling. Her stomach tightened. The windscreen reflected the light, concealing whoever was inside but she could just about make out what looked like a hi-vis jacket.

"That car's been there a while," she whispered.

Emily followed her gaze, frowning. "You sure?"

The hairs on Maddy's arms stood up. The air was too still, and the street too quiet.

Before she could answer, the engine revved softly, and the car rolled away into the night.

Maddy watched it disappear, a cold certainty settling in her gut.

Not a coincidence. Another warning. And she had no intention of heeding it.

Emily hesitated. "Maddy..."

Maddy exhaled, forcing her shoulders to relax. "It's fine."

"It's really not."

She turned to Emily, her jaw tight. "I know."

Emily shook her head. "Be careful."

Maddy simply nodded, already reaching for her phone as Emily walked away.

Her thumb hovered over Tom Denton's number. Writing something quickly before she hit send. A simple message: *We need to talk. Tomorrow.*

Whatever happened next, she was done waiting.

It was time to go on the offensive.

Chapter Twelve

Maddy sat in the corner of The Magpie Café, staring into the depths of her untouched tea. It had seemed a good idea at the time, but somewhere between ordering it and drinking it, her mind had started churning with warnings and coincidences, reports and dead bodies. The café was busy, with the warm scent of fresh bread and frying fish wrapping around her, but she felt disconnected from it. The hum of conversation, the clinking of cutlery against plates, it all blurred into the background.

Across from her, one of her few old Whitby friends Lauren Mills took a sip of her latte, one perfectly shaped eyebrow arching. "You're here, but you're not really here, are you?" she said, setting her cup down with a knowing smirk.

Maddy forced a small smile. "Sorry. My mind's just elsewhere."

"No kidding," Lauren said. "I've been talking about this security job in Leeds for the last five minutes, and you haven't heard a word."

Maddy exhaled, leaning back in her seat. She and Lauren had started out as rookies together, but while Maddy had stayed with the police, Lauren had left a few years ago to start her own private security business. She looked good, relaxed in a way Maddy hadn't felt in years.

"Sorry," Maddy said again. "It's been a long few weeks."

Lauren studied her, a frown tugging at her lips. "How bad is it?"

Maddy hesitated. She trusted Lauren, but this wasn't a simple conversation. "Bad enough that I don't get lunches like this any more."

Lauren sighed. "You know, you could always jump ship. I could use someone like you. The money's better, and you wouldn't have to deal with...*whatever* this is."

Maddy smirked. "Tempting. But I'm not done here yet."

Lauren shook her head, leaning back. "That's what I always liked about you, Mads. Stubborn as hell. But seriously, you look like you're running on fumes. You should take a step back."

There it was. It wasn't just her own mam who was giving her this advice then. Maddy tapped her fingers against her cup, the warmth seeping into her skin but not quite reaching the rest of her. "Can't. If I do, people get hurt."

Lauren's smirk faded. "It's about that case, isn't it? The one you won't talk about?"

On a few of their phone conversations she'd touched on the subject. Nothing more. Now, she simply nodded and thankfully, Lauren didn't push any further. Maybe it was professional courtesy on Lauren's part. Maybe her friend knew that Maddy would talk when she needed to.

Maddy was about to pivot the conversation to the handsome man she'd seen on Lauren's social media when her phone buzzed against the table. Maddy glanced at the screen, Emily. Immediately, her stomach clenched.

Lauren's eyes flicked to Maddy's face, reading the shift in her expression instantly. "That work?"

Maddy gave a tight nod. "Yeah."

Lauren exhaled, setting her cup down. "Then take it. You've looked like you've been waiting for a call all day."

Maddy didn't argue. She pushed back her chair and stood, flashing Lauren a grateful look. "Back in a sec."

She stepped outside, pressing the phone to her ear as the cool sea air wrapped around her. The faint cries of gulls mixed with the chatter of tourists wandering the cobbled streets.

"What have you got?" Maddy asked, already knowing Emily wouldn't call unless it was important.

Emily's voice was sharp with urgency. "Something, at least. A bloke who used to work with Daniel Cross. A retired paramedic called Neil Hampton. Says he's got a story we'll want to hear."

Maddy's heartbeat kicked up. "How reliable is he?"

"Dunno, but he didn't want to talk over the phone. Said he'd meet us at The Dolphin later this afternoon or evening."

Maddy didn't hesitate. "I'll meet you at the station in ten." The station was the safest place to regroup, to go over their next steps with some level of control. If Neil really had something on Cross, they needed to handle this properly...meticulously. The last thing they could afford was scaring off a lead that might be the only solid connection they had. "I'll pull the files on Daniel's old paramedic shifts while I wait for you," she added, already turning back into the cafe. "We need to know exactly where he was when those deaths happened. See you in a bit."

She ended the call and weaved through the tables to where Lauren was sitting, watching her approach.

"Does that mean you have to go?" her friend asked, reaching for her bag.

Maddy gave her an apologetic look and nodded. "I'm so sorry. I owe you lunch and maybe even dinner."

Lauren smiled and waved away her apology.

"It's fine, honestly," she stood and gave her a squeeze. "Go and catch your bad guy."

* * *

The Dolphin was a small, dimly lit pub overlooking the harbour. The smell of salt and ale mixed with the faint scent of fried food. Maddy and Emily arrived early, sliding into a booth near the door where they could see everyone coming and going.

Maddy ordered two lemonades, though neither of them took a sip. The condensation on the glasses dripped onto the worn wooden table, forming small, uneven pools. The pub was quiet for a Saturday evening, the low hum of conversation blending with the occasional clink of glasses behind the bar. A couple of regulars sat near the window, muttering to each other over their pints, but Maddy barely registered them. Her fingers tapped against her knee, her eyes flicking toward the door every few seconds.

She checked her watch. Five minutes past the meeting time.

Ten minutes.

Fifteen.

The unease inside her grew, twisting in her stomach like a vice. Across from her, Emily shifted in her seat, her own posture tense.

"He should be here by now," she murmured, voice low.

Maddy inhaled sharply, her gut telling her exactly what she didn't want to admit.

Something wasn't right.

Then, her phone buzzed. Unknown number.

She answered it. "Sergeant Frost."

A male voice on the other end, a colleague, clipped and professional, but carrying an undercurrent of urgency. "Sergeant

Frost? We've got a situation. You need to get down to Eshton Road immediately."

Maddy straightened, fingers tightening around her phone. "What's happened?"

A brief hesitation. Then, "Man found dead in his flat. Name's Neil Hampton. Possible suicide. But...something's off."

Maddy's stomach dropped. Across the table, Emily was already watching her closely, sensing the shift in atmosphere. "We're on our way," she replied, before ending the call and meeting Emily's expectant gaze.

"It's Hampton," she said, her voice low but firm. "He's dead. Suicide."

The constable furrowed her brows and shook her head. "No. Not a suicide. A Silencing."

* * *

Neil Hampton's flat smelled of dust, cigarette smoke, and something stale underneath it all. The kind of smell that clung to the walls, woven deep into the fabric of old furniture. Like many first responders that Maddy knew, it appeared that Neil's private life was a shambles. His flat was tidy in a liveable sort of way, but there was a mess of takeaway cartons in the sink, and dust on the surfaces. Nurses and police officers didn't get to spend a lot of time at home, Maddy considered. The air was thick, unmoving, the radiator still humming faintly despite the chill that seeped through the small windows.

A uniformed officer stood by the door, scribbling into his notebook, while another mumbled into his radio near the hallway. The crime scene log lay open on a side table, listing the time of entry, the responding officers, and forensic personnel en route. The whole place felt too still, too arranged, like a stage set before the final curtain call.

Hampton's body was slumped in an armchair, his head tilted slightly to the side, eyes half-lidded. A whisky glass lay overturned beside him, its contents pooling into the grain of the wooden table. Pills were scattered across the coffee table, too many to count at first glance.

A note was placed neatly next to the glass. *Couldn't live with the guilt. I'm sorry.*

Maddy didn't buy it for a second.

She moved further into the room, scanning the scene. Everything was too clean, too controlled. No sign of distress beyond the forced narrative laid out in front of them. No struggle, except...

She crouched beside the body, narrowing her eyes at a faint mark on Hampton's wrist, the kind left by someone being forcibly restrained. A sliver of bruising beneath the surface.

"He struggled," she muttered.

Emily, standing just behind her, exhaled sharply. "Jesus. If he was about to talk, then..."

"Someone shut him up first," Maddy finished, her jaw tightening.

Emily shifted, taking in the staged suicide. "We were too late. What do we do?"

Maddy clenched her fists. "This wasn't guilt. This was a warning. And it worked. We're back to square one."

* * *

Back at the station, Harper was furious. "You had a meeting set up with a man who's now dead, and you didn't think to inform me?" His voice was low but razor-sharp, each syllable carrying the weight of his frustration.

Maddy fought to keep her voice steady, though her hands curled into fists at her sides. "We're informing you now, sir.

We just didn't have time. He was scared. And now we know why."

Harper let out a slow exhale, then leaned forward, bracing his forearms against the desk. "And now he's dead. Maybe you should start asking yourself why people around you keep turning up that way."

The words landed like a gut punch. Maddy felt the air shift, as if the room had suddenly become smaller. She wanted to snap back, to tell him this wasn't her fault, but a small, unwelcome doubt curled in the pit of her stomach. Was she really helping this case, or was she making it worse?

Instead of answering, she turned on her heel and strode out, jaw tight. The moment she stepped into the corridor, she sucked in a breath, pressing her fingers to her temples. The fluorescent lights above hummed, her pulse thrumming alongside them.

Emily caught up within seconds, matching her pace as they walked through the station. "We'll get him, Maddy. We will."

Maddy nodded, but her throat was too tight to answer. She kept walking, forcing one foot in front of the other.

She just didn't know if they'd still be standing when they did.

Chapter Thirteen

Maddy sat at her desk, staring at the murder board in front of her.

Murder Board. She had always thought it a gruesome, gory sort of a name that belonged in TV shows. But now, with the ID photos of several victims rapidly filling this case already, Maddy guessed the name was pretty apt.

The station hummed around her, phones ringing, conversations overlapping, the distant clatter of keyboards. Life went on, but inside her head, there was only static. The red string connecting names and faces seemed more like a tangled mess than an organised web of evidence. She had all the pieces. She just couldn't make them fit fast enough.

She rubbed a hand over her face, the tension knotting in her forehead. She'd barely slept, barely eaten. Her brain was running on caffeine and sheer bloody-mindedness, and even that was wearing thin. The chair opposite hers scraped against the floor, and a mug was placed in front of her.

"You need to step back a minute," Emily said, dropping into the chair and stretching out her legs. "You're spiralling."

Step back, step back. Why is everyone telling me that at the moment? She thought a little irritably. She didn't look up. "We're running out of time."

Emily exhaled, clearly ready to argue, but before she could, the station phone rang. One of the desk officers called across the room. "Frost! Call for you, someone asking for you by name."

Maddy's stomach knotted. The last time someone had called her directly, it had been a warning. She hesitated before pushing herself up and making her way over to the phone. Emily watched her closely, but Maddy ignored it. She picked up the receiver. "Detective Sergeant Frost."

A woman's voice crackled through the line, thin and urgent. "Detective Frost? It's Gillian Longstaff. I... I've been going through Peter's things. I found his journal, and I think you need to see this. Please."

* * *

Maddy met Gillian Longstaff at a café in the town centre. The place was busy with the lunch crowd, but the noise barely touched their small table in the corner. Gillian sat with her hands curled around a cup of untouched tea, her fingers pale and tense. She looked exhausted, the kind of tired that settled into the bones and refused to leave.

Maddy studied her carefully, noting the slight tremble in her hands, the way her eyes darted towards the door as if expecting someone to walk in and end this conversation before it even started. "You said you found Peter's journal," Maddy prompted gently. "What did it say?"

Gillian's fingers tightened around the cup, her knuckles turning white as if she needed the warmth of the ceramic to steady herself.

"My husband, Peter...he was fine. At least, he should have been."

Her voice wavered slightly, and she took a deep breath, as if steadying herself before diving into waters she wasn't sure she could swim in. She lifted the cup to her lips but didn't drink, setting it back down with a barely audible clink. Her gaze darted past Maddy's shoulder, scanning the room.

Maddy didn't push. She'd seen this kind of fear before, the kind that took root deep, wrapping itself around a person's sense of safety until they weren't sure what was real and what was imagined. The kind of fear that made you question everything.

Gillian swallowed, the muscles in her throat tightening.

Sarah pushed a small leather journal across the table. "I found this in his desk drawer last night. After you came to visit, I couldn't stop thinking about what you asked—whether Peter was afraid of that paramedic, Daniel." Her voice dropped. "He was terrified. Look."

She opened the journal to a marked page, her finger trembling as she pointed to Peter's handwriting. "He documented everything. The sleepless nights, the feeling of being watched, the sense that someone had been in our house." Her eyes met Maddy's. "And he wrote the same thing over and over: 'He isn't done with me yet.'"

Maddy leaned forward slightly, her tone gentle but firm.

"What kind of things?"

Gillian's jaw clenched. "He'd wake up in the middle of the night, swearing someone had been in the room. He started avoiding certain roads, certain places, said he felt like he was being followed. He stopped sleeping properly, and jumped at every noise. It was like something had crawled under his skin, something he couldn't shake. He kept saying the same thing over and over again."

Maddy felt the pulse of adrenaline in her veins. "What did he say?"

Gillian's breath was unsteady, her eyes finally meeting Maddy's.

"That it wasn't over. That Daniel Cross wasn't done with him yet."

* * *

Back at the station, Maddy sat at her desk, flipping through Peter Longstaff's autopsy report. The clinical detachment of the words on the page clashed with the gnawing unease in her gut. The report was routine, almost too neat, and just like all the others. Nothing suspicious. Nothing unusual. Just another death with no obvious foul play. Too clean. Too convenient.

The station around her was a low hum of activity, phones ringing, the occasional burst of laughter from another unit, the distant scrape of chairs being dragged across the floor. Life going on as if she wasn't sitting here, trying to find the flaw in a dead man's last moments.

Dr. Patel appeared in the doorway, arms crossed over his chest, a takeaway coffee cup dangling from one hand. "You called? Just finished a meeting with one of your colleagues."

Maddy barely glanced up, still staring at the report in front of her. "Ah, perfect timing. Yes. I need another pair of eyes on this."

He stepped inside, setting his coffee on the edge of her cluttered desk. "That bad?"

She exhaled, sliding the file toward him. "Yes, in the sense that nothing is bad. Peter Longstaff. Forty-six, no prior heart issues, no red flags in his medical history, and yet he drops dead from a heart attack a month after surviving a near-fatal crash. Doesn't sit right."

Dr. Patel perched on the edge of the desk, flipping through

the report with his usual careful precision. His brows knitted together after a moment. "Wait. This is interesting."

Maddy straightened, her pulse picking up. "What?"

Patel pulled out his laptop, resting it on some papers before quickly accessing his files. He began cross-referencing reports, his frown deepening. "Look at this. Adrenaline levels. Through the roof. Right before death."

Maddy leaned in, scanning the numbers. The data was clear, just like the other victims, Peter's body was flooded with adrenaline before he died. No external trigger. No logical cause.

"It's like his body thought he was running for his life before he died," she thought aloud.

Dr. Patel sat back, arms crossed. "Like he knew it was coming."

Maddy's grip on the edge of the desk tightened. The walls of coincidence were closing in. And she had no intention of letting them hold.

* * *

Maddy stormed into Harper's office, slamming the file onto his desk. "I keep telly you. This isn't coincidence. It's a pattern."

Harper exhaled sharply. "You're asking me to believe a man can scare people to death, Frost."

"No, I'm asking you to look at the bloody evidence. He's doing something to them. We just don't know what yet."

Harper pinched the bridge of his nose. "Even if you're right, we've got no cause of death, no proof, and no solid link to Daniel Cross beyond speculation."

Maddy shook her head. "I need a warrant. Let me search his residence"

"No." Harper's mouth was a grim line. "And it's not me who signs off on that anyway, and you know it. That has to go before a judge, and it'll be my neck on the line for submitting a warrant with *at best* circumstantial evidence. You can't have it."

Maddy let out a frustrated cough, turning in place to pace the room. She had to make him see. This was the only way.

For Dad.

She turned back, and did something she never did. Not with Harper, and certainly not with any man. "Boss, *please*. People are dying. More people *are going* to die. But we can stop it. I know we can. I believe in us, I believe in this force, and…damn it…I think Whitby deserves better than to have this lunatic threatening it!"

Harper studied her, his expression unreadable. Then he sighed, rubbing his temples. "You've got 48 hours, Frost. Find something solid, or you drop this."

Maddy nodded, already turning on her heel. "I won't need that long."

* * *

She pulled up outside her mother's cottage later that night, exhaustion pressing down on her like a lead weight. The headlights cut through the darkness, illuminating the familiar front door, but for the first time, it didn't feel like home. It felt like a checkpoint, a place to catch her breath before plunging back into the fight.

As she killed the engine, she sat for a moment, gripping the steering wheel, trying to slow the thoughts tumbling over themselves in her mind. Her muscles ached, her eyes burned, and all she wanted was a few hours of dreamless sleep. But sleep wasn't something she could afford, not when every step forward felt like a trap waiting to be sprung.

She forced herself out of the car, stretching her stiff limbs as she approached the cottage. The small garden was still, the porch light flickering slightly as the sea breeze toyed with it. She reached for her keys, but something made her pause. A shift in the air, a subtle wrongness that she couldn't place.

And then she saw it, a small, folded piece of paper on the doorstep, stark white against the dark stone. Her breath catching in her throat as she bent down, fingers brushing against the rough surface as she picked it up. The street behind her was empty, silent except for the distant crash of waves against the cliffs.

Unfolding the note, she read the single line scrawled across it in jagged, hurried script:

You're looking in the wrong place.

A chill ran down her spine. The message wasn't just a warning, it was a challenge. An invitation. Daniel Cross wasn't just watching. He was guiding her, nudging her toward something she hadn't yet seen.

And that terrified her more than anything.

Chapter Fourteen

You're looking in the wrong place.

Maddy sat at the kitchen table, staring down at the small piece of paper between her fingers. She had barely slept, her mind running in relentless circles around the message, turning it over, dissecting it, trying to pull meaning from something that felt more like a taunt than a clue.

Come on, she pushed her tired brain to work a little faster. This was a clue, right? What did they say at the academy? Everything told a story.

She studied the handwriting. It was scrawled in jagged, uneven loops and lines, the ink slightly smudged.

Nervous? Unhinged? Or was it written in haste? Whatever the reason for the uneven writing was, Maddy didn't find anything about it comforting.

Across from her, Claire placed two steaming mugs of tea on the table and lowered herself into the chair opposite. She didn't say anything at first, just studied her daughter with the quiet patience of a mother who had spent too many years watching someone she loved wear themselves thin. The soft light of the kitchen made the lines on her face more pronounced, deep furrows carved from years of worry, of nights spent waiting for Maddy to come home from a job that had always taken too much from her.

"I know that look," Claire finally said, her voice warm but edged with quiet exhaustion. She wrapped her hands around her mug, her fingers absently tracing patterns on the ceramic. "You're about to do something reckless."

Maddy exhaled sharply, forcing herself to look up. The concern in her mother's eyes twisted something in her chest. Claire had already lost a husband. Now, she was watching her daughter spiral further into a case that was starting to feel like a noose tightening around her throat.

"I can't just sit here, Mam." Maddy pushed the note aside, rubbing her temples. "He's always ahead of me. Every time I think I've got him boxed in, he slips away."

Her mam sighed, taking a slow sip of her tea before setting the mug down. "And what happens when you get too close, love?"

Maddy clenched her jaw. "Then I finish it."

Claire reached across the table, resting a gentle hand over Maddy's. The touch was grounding, but it also carried weight, a mother's unspoken plea. "I know you think you have to do this alone. But you don't. And you don't have to do it at the expense of yourself."

Maddy swallowed, throat tight. She wanted to tell her mother that this was different, that this wasn't just another case. But Claire already knew that. She could see it in the way she held herself, in the way she kept looking at Maddy like she was trying to memorise her face, just in case.

For a brief moment, Maddy let herself lean into the warmth of her mother's touch before pulling away, forcing herself back to the reality of the case. "I need to change tactics."

Claire arched a brow. "And by 'change tactics,' you mean?"

Maddy pushed back from the table, standing. "I need to make him feel the heat. If he thinks no one's watching, he'll keep moving. But if I put him in the spotlight..."

Claire exhaled slowly, already knowing where this was going. "You're going to the journalist, aren't you?" Maddy had already shared with her mother her reconnecting with Tom. Her mother had raised her eyebrow in that way she had, but hadn't said anything.

Maddy didn't answer, just grabbed her coat from the back of the chair and slung it over her shoulders. Claire watched her with something between resignation and quiet understanding.

"Just...promise me you won't do something you can't take back."

Maddy hesitated at the doorway, turning back for a second. "I'll be careful."

But they both knew it was a lie.

* * *

She parked outside Tom Denton's office, staring at the building sandwiched between a bookshop and a bakery. The last time she'd been here, she'd pulled him into the chaos. He'd already helped her once, and paid for it. Coming back to him now felt like asking too much, but she had no other choice.

For better or worse, that only person who could help her was Tom.

She stepped inside and the man himself looked up from his desk, raising an eyebrow, his expression unreadable. It was understandable if he was going to be angry with her, Maddy thought. Tom wore a bandage across his forehead from the previous attack, and the other side of his face was deeply purpled with bruising.

"Well, well," he said, leaning back in his chair. "Didn't think

I'd be seeing you again so soon, Mads." He leaned forward, elbows on the desk. "I can't believe you're still messing around with this case. It's fucking dangerous."

She pulled a file from her bag and slid it across the desk. "I feel like this is my last chance to make sure people know who Daniel Cross really is."

His lighter expression vanished, replaced by something heavier. He didn't immediately open the file. Instead, he sighed, rubbing the back of his neck. "And I'm guessing your boss wouldn't sign off on this."

Maddy met his gaze. "Which is why you're the only one who knows I'm here."

Tom studied her for a moment, the weight of past wounds and unfinished words hanging in the air. There was a flicker of something in his expression, hesitation, maybe even hurt. The last time she'd walked into his office, it had been about the case. But before that? Before Whitby had turned into a graveyard of unsolved mysteries for her, there had been that *thing* between them. He didn't mention it, and neither did she...but the ghost of opportunities lost and untaken chances hovered between them.

Would we have been good together? Would we have worked? Maddy couldn't know the answer to that. If anything, it would have been intense. Their personalities were too similar, too stubborn, and too opinionated.

But sometimes it was nice to speculate, and she could see the same thoughts deep in the way he looked back at her.

Tom's expression shifted from mild intrigue to something far more serious. He thumbed through the documents, case notes, victim lists, connections that no one had pieced together publicly yet. "Jesus," he muttered. He rubbed a hand across his jaw, glancing up at her. "If this goes live, he'll know someone's onto him."

Maddy swallowed, holding his gaze. "That's the idea."

Tom exhaled sharply, tossing the pen he'd been fidgeting with onto the desk. "You really don't do half-measures, do you?" His voice was quieter now, but she caught the edge of something deeper in it. Worry. Frustration. "Mads, last time I stuck my neck out for you, I got smashed up. If I do this, I need to know you're not walking into something you can't come back from."

Her throat tightened. She had no guarantees, no reassurances. Just the same drive that had always pushed her forward, even when it burned her in the process. "I wouldn't be here if I had another choice."

Tom sighed, rubbing his forehead before nodding. "Alright, fine. But if this backfires—"

"It won't."

She stood, already heading for the door. But before she could leave, Tom's voice stopped her.

"Be careful, Mads."

She turned slightly, their eyes meeting for just a moment too long. Then she walked out.

* * *

By the next morning, the article was already live. Tom worked quickly.

Is a Serial Killer Hiding in Plain Sight?

The headline was bold, but not outright accusatory and the article wove together the pattern Maddy had been tracking, highlighting the suspicious deaths without directly naming Daniel. It was just enough to plant doubt in the right people's minds, enough to make those who had encountered him before take notice.

By the time she made it to the station, the article had spread. People were talking. And Harper was waiting for her.

He stormed into the room, the Whitby Gazette clenched so tightly in his fist that it crumpled along the edges. His face was thunderous, eyes dark with fury as he strode straight for her desk.

"Tell me you had nothing to do with this," he demanded, his voice sharp, controlled, but barely. He slammed his hand on the desk. "You went behind my back and fed your journalist friend details of our investigation? That's enough to get you suspended." He leaned closer, lowering his voice. "The only reason you're still on this is because I'm covering you. But you don't get another free pass. One more slip and you're off the case."

Maddy didn't flinch, though she could feel Emily shifting uncomfortably beside her. The tension in the room crackled, thick and heavy. As far as she'd seen, Harper rarely lost his temper like this, but she'd known this confrontation was coming the moment she'd seen the article go live.

She folded her arms, keeping her expression unreadable. "I didn't leak department information. It's all public record."

Harper laughed, but it wasn't amusement, just a short, brittle bark of disbelief. "Don't patronise me, Frost. You and I both know what this is. You took a calculated risk to stir the pot, and now it's boiling over."

He stepped in closer, looming without raising his voice, the kind of anger that simmered just under the surface. "You made Daniel Cross feel the heat. You think that's clever? You think that's going to make him slip up? All it's done is put a target on your back, and now, apparently, on your mother's too."

Maddy stiffened at the mention of her mum, but she didn't let it show on her face.

Harper's voice dropped. "You want to go down swinging, that's your prerogative. But dragging innocent people into your crusade? That's not policing. That's arrogance. And it'll get someone killed."

The room was thick with tension. Emily didn't move. No one else spoke. Maddy could feel every pair of eyes on her, but all she saw was Harper's grim expression and the weight behind his words.

She didn't flinch. Didn't even blink. "You gave me 48 hours. This is what progress looks like."

Harper's mouth twisted, something like disappointment flickering across his face. "You'd better be right, Frost. Because if you're wrong, it won't just be your badge on the line. It'll be someone else's life."

* * *

That evening, Maddy was pulling off her boots when her phone rang.

She glanced at the screen and frowned, answering immediately. "Mam?"

There was a pause before Claire's voice came through, laced with unease. Instantly, Maddy knew that something was wrong. Her mam wasn't usually like this. She was known for being breezy and direct in her phone calls. "Maddy...I just got a phone call. I thought it was a wrong number, but they didn't say anything. Just silence."

Maddy's stomach twisted. "Did you recognise the number?"

"No caller ID."

Her grip tightened around the phone. The room felt suddenly colder. Her mother was trying to brush it off, but Maddy heard the slight tremor in her voice.

"It was probably just a prank," Claire said, attempting reassurance.

Maddy exhaled slowly. "No, Mam. It wasn't."

She didn't say the rest out loud. She didn't have to. Claire wasn't just a bystander any more. She was part of this now.

Later that day, Maddy sat in her car outside her mam's house, watching, waiting. The street was quiet.

Too quiet.

She drummed her fingers against the steering wheel, scanning the darkness. Every shadow felt heavier, every movement was suspicious. A figure moved near the edge of the garden, and her breath caught, but it was just the neighbour, dragging his bins out to the pavement.

Still, she couldn't shake the feeling. Exhaustion clawed at every inch of her and there was a tiny part deep down that could see how irrational this was. But she was going to take on any 'what ifs'. Especially if it involved her own mother.

Her phone buzzed. An unknown number. A text.

That was a mistake.

Maddy stared at the words, a chill creeping up her spine.

Daniel Cross had seen the article.

And now, he was watching her back.

Chapter Fifteen

Maddy hadn't slept. The anonymous text, *That was a mistake*, still echoed in her mind like a bell struck too hard. She'd stayed parked outside her mam's cottage all night, wrapped in her coat and one of her dad's old sleeping bags, the engine idling only long enough to keep the windscreen clear. The sky was turning a bruised grey, the kind of early morning hush that made every creak of the car feel louder than it should.

She'd been sipping lukewarm coffee from a flask when a soft knock at the window made her jump. Her mother stood outside, wrapped in a dressing gown, her breath fogging in the cold. Maddy rolled the window down a crack.

"You've been out here most of the night," Claire sighed, her tone caught between concern and weary exasperation. "You'll get ill."

"I can't have you hurt, mam," Maddy muttered, rubbing her eyes.

Claire bent down slightly, voice softening. "If this creep wanted to do something, he would have already. You're worrying yourself sick."

Maddy stared straight ahead, visions of the day she lost her dad flashing in her mind. The heartache, the overwhelming urge to scream from the inside out. "I can't lose you too."

Her mother sighed and opened the car door, crouching so they were level. She cupped Maddy's cheek with her hand, warm, familiar. Grounding. "Then catch him. But do it the right way."

* * *

Emily was already glued to her monitor, fingers dancing over the keyboard, a half-drunk can of Coke teetering on the edge of her desk, when Maddy arrived at the station.

She'd tip-toed past DI Harper's office, hoping he didn't notice her late arrival. The last thing she wanted was to give him another reason to haul her in and give her a telling-off. Their relationship was already fractured after the article had gone out.

"You remember Ellie Rogers, right?" Emily asked her without looking up.

"The nurse," Maddy replied, stripping off her coat. She draped it over the back of her chair. "Yeah, I remember."

Emily turned the screen towards her. "She's back. Registered for a tenancy under her sister's name. A flat out by the viaduct."

Maddy arched an eyebrow. "Why now?"

"No idea. But if she's resurfaced, she might be ready to talk."

She couldn't pass up the opportunity to squeeze every last bit of information Ellie had before she had a chance to disappear again.

"We're not waiting," Maddy said pointing to the screen. "Get your coat."

* * *

Ellie's flat sat at the top of a narrow staircase, the kind that creaked with every step and smelt faintly of mildew and old varnish. The building was a squat, grimy block of flats wedged between a boarded-up corner shop and a fish bar with flickering signage. It was easy to see that the woman didn't have a lot of money, in a town where no one had a whole heap of money. Paint peeled from the walls in long, scabby strips, and a faded notice about noise complaints hung crookedly in the entryway. As Maddy and Emily climbed the stairs, the banister wobbled under Emily's hand, and a lightbulb overhead buzzed weakly, casting shadows that made the narrow corridor feel even more claustrophobic.

They reached the top landing, where a thin strip of worn carpet bunched under their boots. Ellie's door was scratched around the handle, the wood swollen from damp. When Maddy knocked, it was answered not by words but by the hesitant rattle of chains sliding back, the metal sound taut with unease. A narrow gap opened, and through it, a pale, drawn face peered out, eyes wide with distrust.

"Ellie," Maddy said gently, keeping her hands visible and her tone soft. "We just want to talk."

After a pause, then the door opened.

Inside, the place was dim and cramped, and heavy with an atmosphere of despair. The blinds were pulled shut, casting narrow stripes of light across the cluttered carpet. Ellie looked thinner than either of them remembered. Her hair hung limp, and her eyes darted constantly, like a cornered animal.

She sat opposite them on a sunken sofa, lighting a cigarette with shaking fingers. The smoke curled around her like a shield.

"I shouldn't be talking to you," she whispered.

Maddy leaned forward. "Ellie, people are dying."

"They've been dying for years," she threw back, her voice brittle. "And I should've said something sooner."

Emily stayed quiet, letting Maddy lead.

"You worked with Daniel Cross. You saw something, didn't you?"

Ellie exhaled, smoke trailing out of her nose from the constant chain of nervy cigarettes that moved from packet to mouth to ashtray and round again. "He visited them. The patients. Even after they were discharged. Showed up at their homes. Sat with them in hospital rooms even when they didn't remember why he was there."

Maddy's stomach turned. "Why?"

Ellie stared at her ashtray. "I asked him once. He said, 'Because they're not supposed to be here.'"

Emily sucked in a breath. "He wasn't saving lives."

"He was deciding who deserved to keep them," Maddy finished.

Ellie nodded slowly, drawing hard on her cigarette. "That's when I knew I had to get out. I put in for a transfer the week after he said that. Two days later, the paperwork vanished. HR said I'd never filed anything."

Emily sat forward. "You think he intercepted it?"

Ellie shrugged, but her voice was hollow. "I don't think. I know. That's why I left the whole damn job. I packed a bag, moved in with my sister, and tried to forget everything but couldn't. Not when people kept dying."

Maddy's heart twisted. "Why didn't you come forward then?"

"Would you have believed me if I did?" Ellie snapped. "Would anyone? He's a local damn hero. He's saved lives and got commendations for it. But behind closed doors? He watches. Waits. And when it's time, he takes."

For a moment, no one spoke. The air in the flat felt even heavier than it had minutes ago. Ellie reached over and stubbed out her cigarette, her hand trembling as she ground it into the ashtray. "You're already in deeper than I ever was. Just don't wait too long. If you start seeing him pop up, it's already over."

Maddy opened her mouth to reply, but the nurse cut her a look, sharp, afraid. Then her eyes softened, flicking away toward the curtained window.

"There was one," she said suddenly, like the name had surfaced from a fog. Her voice lowered. "Louis Wren. Survived a bad crash two months ago. Daniel visited him three times after he was discharged. Once, I found Daniel sitting outside his rehab centre for hours and when I asked what he was doing, all he said was he was making sure fate didn't miss him twice."

The words landed like a stone in Maddy's chest. She glanced at Emily, who was already reaching for her tablet. They didn't need to say anything. Not any more.

"Address?" Maddy asked, voice low but urgent. Ellie scribbled it down on a scrap of paper, hands still trembling.

As they stood, she didn't follow them to the door. Instead, she sat back on the sofa, curling into herself, as though she was already halfway back into hiding.

* * *

Louis Wren's flat was in an older block near Green Lane, a narrow backstreet off the beaten track on Whitby's east side. The building stood hunched behind a low brick wall, its render mottled with moss and salt spray carried up from the harbour. Bins clustered by the alleyway gave off the sour tang of rot, and a faded For Sale sign creaked in the morning breeze. A light frost clung to the privet hedge and the parked cars, brittle and pale in the thin light. Across the rooftops, the Abbey ruins loomed in silhouette.

Maddy and Emily stepped out of the car, boots crunching on gravel. Maddy's stomach knotted. Everything about the place felt wrong, like it was holding its breath. The curtains of the upper flat hung closed, still. But it wasn't the stillness that bothered her. It was the quiet. Even Whitby had sounds, gulls, distant traffic, the clink of glass from cafés getting ready to open. But up here, it was just dead air.

"Front door's open," Emily whispered, nodding toward the crooked entranceway.

Maddy raised a hand to stop her, her other drawing her torch. She pushed the door slowly. The air inside was wrong, too still, heavy with something that didn't belong. The living room was neat, too neat.

Louis Wren lay slumped in an armchair, his eyes wide open, frozen in place. A single piece of paper was pinned to his chest with a metal paper-clip.

Too late, Frost.

Maddy stared, her heart pounding.

Emily knelt beside the body, checking for a pulse she already knew wasn't there. "He's been dead for hours," she breathed. "I'm going to call this in."

Maddy couldn't tear her eyes away from the note. "Daniel knew we were coming," she said. "He's been watching our every move."

The silence was deafening. Every tick of the clock felt like a taunt. Emily rose, brushing her hands off before she pulled out her phone. "We've found a body, unresponsive male, dead-on-arrival, Green Lane..." she spoke the bureaucratic codes and ciphers that meant they were too late into the handset.

Maddy stayed still for a moment, her phone in her lap, the weight of Louis Wren's death still sinking in. That note, with those four words, burned in her mind like acid.

She stepped outside for air. The cold hit her lungs hard, but it was grounding. Her fingers curled into fists. Enough was enough.

She turned and looked back at the flat, Louis Wren's final resting place, just another casualty in a string of deliberate, orchestrated deaths. Her stomach clenched. Whatever this was, he wasn't done playing and she wasn't just going to sit around waiting for his next move.

The sound of sirens echoed in the distance and she took a deep breath. There was only one thing she could do, wasn't there? She was going to force his hand.

Chapter Sixteen

Maddy arrived at the station sometime after five, her coat still damp from the cold drizzle that had followed them all the way from Louis Wren's grim little flat. The sky outside had turned a dull steel, the kind that pressed in low and slow like a warning. The station lights burned too bright after hours in dim hallways and silence. Maddy blinked against the sudden harshness of it, her head pounding in time with the dull throb behind her eyes.

The door shut behind her with a soft clunk. It was quieter than usual, not the hush of night, not yet, but the lull that settled when half the shift had gone home and the other half were counting down the minutes. Still, as she walked past the desks on her floor, a few heads turned. Not overt, not dramatic. Just the slight lift of brows, a shift in posture. She wasn't just one of them any more, not tonight.

Maddy had received Harper's message on the way over. It was formal and clipped, and nothing like how her superior talked himself.

That's because he's covering his arse, Maddy thought.

Harper didn't want a misconduct suit or an internal complaint filed against him.

'*Detective Sergeant Madeleine Frost. You have been removed from current investigation #W8370. All materials related to the investigation are to be handed in immediately, and you are forbidden from accessing them, contacting suspects, victims, or persons unknown connected with the case.*'

"Thanks, boss," Maddy muttered under her breath as she strode forward. She didn't say anything to any of her colleagues. Instead she walked the corridor like she had countless times before and deposited her report into Harper's in-tray. Thank fuck he wasn't in his office. She couldn't deal with the confrontation. Not tonight. She hesitated, letting her fingertips brush the edge of the top sheet. The words blurred in front of her, dates, names, and events recorded with a detached precision that didn't match the scene, which was still stuck behind her eyes.

She found Emily in the kitchen, leaning against the back counter with a tea in one hand and her phone in the other. Her coat was off, sleeves rolled, hair scraped back like she'd tried to return to normal and almost managed it. Almost.

Emily glanced up. "Hey. Thought you might not come back in this evening."

Maddy walked in slowly, her shoulders heavy. "I needed to finish the report." She reached for the kettle, refilling it without really thinking.

There was a moment of silence before her colleague let out a long breath, "Harper told the team. About you...being taken off."

Maddy's back stiffened. "Right."

"I thought he'd say it to you direct. But he just...said it like it was procedure. As though you were a misplaced file."

The kettle clicked. Maddy poured the water over a tired-looking teabag and stirred without tasting.

"He's protecting himself," Emily added, more cautiously now. "After the press leak and...after today. People are nervous. Morale's taken a hit."

"I'm not the one who pinned a note to a corpse," Maddy said flatly.

Emily gave a small, humourless laugh. "No. But you're the one rattling the bars."

Maddy leaned against the worktop, her eyes on the wall clock. Each tick sounded too loud.

"He's letting Daniel win."

"No," The detective constable said, stepping closer. "He's scared. And maybe you are too. But you're the only one still willing to push this."

Maddy turned to her. "And I guess now I'm doing it alone."

Emily hesitated. "You're not alone. I'm still here. Just... maybe don't make me choose between you and my job, yeah?"

Maddy gave a weary nod. "No promises."

They stood in silence, the weight of everything pressing in between sips of half-forgotten tea. Then Emily finally said it, softly, like it hurt to admit: "You knew it was coming. But that doesn't make it feel any less like a punch."

Maddy's throat went dry. "No. It doesn't."

The road back to her mam's cottage passed in a blur of grey hedgerows and rain-slicked tarmac. By the time Maddy pulled up outside, the sky had begun to bruise at the edges with dusk. Lights were already on in the front windows, casting a warm glow against the gathering dark.

Claire opened the door before she could even knock.

"You should've told me about that Louis Wren," she said, arms folded. "Another death, Mads?"

Maddy stepped inside, stamping the damp from her boots. "I didn't want to drag you in further than you already are."

Her mam raised an eyebrow. "You dragged the whole bloody town in when you went to the press."

"It was the only way to make him show himself."

"And it worked?" she asked, a tone lingering at the end of her question.

Maddy paused. "Yes. Just not the way I'd hoped."

For a moment, they stood in silence. Then her mother's shoulders dropped. "It's not about being right, love. It's about being safe. Come on in. I just need to pop upstairs and get my phone."

Maddy stepped through into the kitchen, shaking off her coat, but something stopped her mid-step. The dining room light was on.

Not something entirely unusual, but the room was rarely used these days. She had memories of her father sitting there doing his work. Late nights pouring through notes and cases. Since then, it was more of a decorative room. Her mam would only use it when she hosted any guests and the posh dinner plates came out.

She hadn't hosted in a long while.

Maddy turned the corner to switch the light off, and froze.

Her father's old leather notebook lay open on the dining table. Surrounding it were pages, loose sheets filled with his familiar tight script, written in biro and pencil, some faded, some sharp as if written yesterday. Every page laid out with surgical precision, not randomly strewn, but arranged. Curated.

Her chest tightened. She stepped closer, fingertips brushing over the edge of one page. A line of shorthand she recognised immediately. Her dad's. A thought process halfway through. She called up the stairs, voice dry. "Mam? Did you do this?"

Footsteps sounded and Claire came down in slippers,

cardigan pulled tight, phone in hand. She stopped in the doorway of the dining room, brow creased.

"I haven't touched those since we boxed them up after the funeral. They were in that cupboard in the hall under the stairs."

Maddy moved to the front door. Locked. So was the back. There were no signs of a break-in, no shattered glass, And no forced entry. But someone had been here.

"And you didn't notice the light in here was on when you came home, Mam?"

Claire shook her head. "No, love," she answered gesturing to her head. "I went straight up to start dying my greys. I didn't even have a look."

Maddy turned back to the table. Eyes scanning the papers again. Her father had been thorough with his work. Dedicated. And seeing his notes out sent that familiar, old pang of sadness through her. It had been years since she lost her father, but sometimes it still hurt just as it did that day.

Maddy's eye's flickered. She noticed one page slightly apart from the others. She picked it up.

It was a report. Handwritten, dated nearly years ago. A road traffic accident. One name was underlined faintly in pencil: Rob Wren.

Below that, another note: *"Deceased: Rob Wren. Paramedic on scene: D. Cross."*

Her stomach dropped. They weren't here to steal. They were here to remind her what she'd missed.

A mug of cold tea untouched beside her, Maddy sat at the table, surrounded by her dad's past, the ghosts of cases closed, thoughts abandoned, things that never added up.

A couple of hours had passed and her mother had since gone to bed, leaving her alone in the dim dining room with the papers.

One entry detailed a late night accident. The victim had died en route. Her dad's notes were concise, clinical, but a comment stuck out at the bottom.

"Something about the paramedic. Too calm. Didn't log his name right away. Seemed familiar," Maddy circled the line with her pen. Daniel Cross. He had been there. Even back then. It gave her some kind of comfort to know that her dad had seen what she had too. That she wasn't going crazy.

"You've been doing this longer than we thought," she whispered under her breath.

Her notebook lay open beside the files. She scrawled Daniel's name again, hard enough to rip the page.

Daniel Cross wasn't just a killer. He was a ghost that threaded through her own family's past. Maybe even through her father's final days.

The stairs creaked softly. Her mam walked in, eyes still hazy with sleep.

"You're still up?" she asked, looking over her shoulder at what she was doing. "You're chasing ghosts, love."

Maddy didn't look up. "No. He's chasing me. Or Dad. Or whatever Dad knew."

Claire lowered herself into a seat opposite sat opposite. "Then promise me something."

Maddy winced. She could tell her mother was going to ask her to promise something she couldn't. She couldn't give up the case when she was this close. "Mam..."

Her mother let a flash of frustration cross her face. "Madeline Frost," she interrupted firmly. "I know I can't tell you what to do any more, but I need you to at least promise me won't do all of this alone?"

Maddy blinked in surprise. She had imagined her mother would be more demanding, more restrictive. She looked at her for a moment, eyes shadowed. "I...I can't promise that."

Silence stretched long between them.

"If Daniel is digging into the past," she answered, finally. "It means he's not just trying to scare me. He's trying to finish something."

Claire placed a hand over hers and said nothing for a long moment.

Maddy's mind raced. She should tell Harper. Request protection for her mother, maybe a safe house. But that would mean admitting the threats, admitting how personal this had become. Harper would pull her from the case entirely, and Daniel Cross would win.

"You need to leave," Maddy said suddenly, her voice tight. "Go stay with Auntie Louise for a few days. Or book a hotel. Somewhere he can't find you."

Claire's expression hardened. "Absolutely not."

"Mam, please. If he's threatening me, he might come after you. I can't..." Her throat closed around the words. She couldn't lose her mother too.

"I'm not leaving my home because some twisted paramedic is playing mind games," her mam said firmly. "This is our house, Maddy. Your father's house. I won't be driven out of it."

"Then I need to tell Harper. Get you a patrol car outside, protection, something..."

"And what will you tell him? That you've been getting anonymous texts? That you're investigating a case you've probably been told to step back from?" Claire shook her head, her voice softening. "You do what you need to do, love, but I'm not running. And I'm not letting you throw your career away to babysit me."

Maddy wanted to argue, to push harder, but she recognised

that tone. Claire Frost had made up her mind. Her father hadn't raised either of them to run from fights.

"Then promise me you'll be careful," Maddy said, her voice breaking slightly. "Lock the doors. Keep your phone on you. If anything feels wrong, anything at all, you call me."

"I promise," Claire said quietly, squeezing her hand. "But you promise me the same."

* * *

Maddy waited until her mam had gone back up to bed before she continued going through the notes, looking for anything that stood out or might help her with the next steps. She was off the case, but that didn't mean she would stop doing her own research.

She turned over a piece of paper and stopped. A faint pencil circle marked a name at the top: *Neil Hampton*.

She stared at it. The man who had tried to talk. The one who had ended up dead.

Shit. Another piece. Another buried clue. Maddy breathed out, low and steady.

Daniel Cross has been cleaning up the trail for years. But now, it looked like she'd just managed to pick it back up.

Chapter Seventeen

The next morning, the air still carried the essence of the storm that had passed over their sleeping (or in Maddy's case, no-so sleeping) heads. The air still felt heavy, and the damp clung to everything.

Maddy hunched into her coat as she stepped into the side alley off Baxtergate and ducked into the back entrance of Rusty Shears, a tucked-away vintage café where the tables were mismatched, the pastries were slightly burnt at the edges, and the Wi-Fi only worked if you sat near the counter. It was perfect. Out of the way. Unofficial.

Emily was already there, seated to the side beneath an antique mirror, two mugs of coffee in front of her and a battered laptop bag wedged between her knees. She looked up as Maddy slid into the opposite seat.

"You look like death, Sarge," Emily said lightly, pushing one of the cups across.

Maddy wrapped her hands around the warm mug and took a sip. "Didn't sleep. I kept going over my dad's notes. There's something we've missed. Something he saw back then that I'm still not putting together."

Emily pulled her laptop free, flipping it open and nudging aside a sugar packet. "Then let's find it. I've got Daniel Cross' employment history. Took a bit of creative navigating, but I got there. Temporary contracts, locum placements, even a couple of charity stints. Bastard moved around more than a carnival."

The hum of conversation around them was soft, as the café was still quiet this early in the day. A pair of dog walkers were huddled at the front by the window, and a pensioner in a waterproof mac had taken up station near the heater, nursing a mug the size of a small cauldron.

Maddy opened her notebook, already half-filled with names, dates, strings of thoughts that barely made sense to anyone else. She flicked to a blank page. "Alright. Let's start pinning him down."

Emily slid a USB stick into the side of her laptop, and a spreadsheet bloomed to life.

"First confirmed job was in Lancashire, about seventeen years ago. Then a steady drift north and east. Couple of months here, three years there. Mostly stuck to coastal towns or rural areas. Not much in terms of city postings," Emily read.

Maddy tapped her pen against her jaw, eyes flicking across the screen. "Ambulance services in the arse end of nowhere. Less oversight. More freedom." *For a guy like him,* she mentally added.

Emily nodded. "Exactly. Now, here's the interesting bit." She clicked to another tab. "I pulled obituaries and sudden death notices from the same towns during his stints. Most of them looked like natural causes at first glance, accidents, unexplained cardiac arrests, that sort of thing. But then I filtered for names that popped up in local news before the deaths. Survivors."

"You're a fucking genius!" Maddy leaned forward. "And?"

"Well, everywhere he's been, he rescued someone from a

near-death incident... and then that same person died mysteriously days or weeks later. Not always high-profile. Not always reported widely. But it's there. Car crashes. Falls. Near drownings. Overdoses. Even a lightning strike. He saves them first, then they die."

She turned the screen. "Look at this. South Shields, 2013. Man rescued from a boating accident. Praised the paramedics. Found dead in his flat twelve days later. No cause of death recorded beyond 'sudden cardiac failure'. Daniel was stationed there that same summer."

The room felt colder.

Maddy began scribbling locations in her notebook. "This isn't chaos. This is a circuit. A method."

Emily highlighted a row. "He's working through something."

Maddy sat back, rubbing her eyes. "It's not about the rescue. It's the aftermath. The people who lived. He chooses who deserves that second chance."

Emily scrolled through a series of victim photos. "Some of these people look similar. I mean, not twins or anything, but a type. Mid-thirties. Similar build. Dark hair."

Maddy leaned in, her brows pulling together as she studied the images. "It can't be coincidence. Not with him. What if he's not just targeting survivors?"

Emily looked up. "What if it's about familiarity?"

Maddy nodded, remembering her criminal pathology 101. Just as every crime left threads, so every criminal had a type, a reason for what they did...a pattern.

He could be acting out on some pathological obsession, or replaying some old trauma, she thought. "They look similar, you think? You think he's replaying something...or someone? Someone he lost? A long lost love? His mother?"

Emily looked stunned, and Maddy wound her fingers tight around her mug, deep in thought.

"Let's make a note of that," she instructed. "It might be important later."

The detective constable scribbled it down in her notebook and put her pen down. "My gut tells me the more we dig, the sooner we're going to uncover something we really don't like."

Maddy nodded. "You know, I used to think after my dad died that maybe it wasn't an accident. That maybe he saw something. Something that got him killed."

Emily didn't flinch. "Maybe he did, but you have more information than your dad did now. You can put a stop to this."

There was a brief pause.

"Yeah, I can." Maddy nodded, barely. She sat up straighter then, voice steadier. "He's not just playing God, Emily. He thinks fate made a mistake. That it gave second chances to the wrong people. And now he's trying to fix it."

Emily spread a printed map out over the table. Coloured sticky tabs, bits of taped-down paper.

"Based on travel patterns, he might circle back to one of these places soon. Scarborough or Hornsea. Both near the coast. Both where he's worked before."

Maddy studied the map. "He's getting faster. More confident. He wants us to see it now. Because by the time we do, it's already done."

Emily tapped her laptop. "One more thing. This came up on an alert I set. Tessa North. Pulled from the sea three weeks ago. Resuscitated by a paramedic."

Maddy straightened. "Let me guess. Daniel Cross?"

Emily nodded. "She's been home two weeks and lives in Robin Hood's Bay. Alone."

Maddy grabbed her coat. Her voice was tight. "Then let's go and talk to her. This can't wait, as she could be next!"

Chapter Eighteen

The drive into Robin Hood's Bay felt different this time. The first time she and Emily had come here, weeks ago now, it had been just a hunch, a thread dangling at the edge of something they didn't know. But now they knew too much. Now every cobbled alley and salt-stained cottage felt like it was watching them back.

The wind rolled in off the sea, bitter and sharp, pushing low mist along the narrow streets. Shops were shuttered against the season, chalkboards smudged with yesterday's specials, fairy lights left unplugged. Maddy's boots crunched against the wet gravel as they stepped out near the Old Chapel and Emily pulled her scarf tighter.

"This place gives me the creeps even when it's out of season," she whispered.

Maddy tried a tired smile. "Perfect place for a killer to hide, I guess?"

Tessa North's cottage sat near the bottom end of Chapel Street, tucked in the crook of a short curve before the slope down to the sea wall. It was narrow, two floors and had whitewashed brick with blue window frames. A faded lifebuoy hung on the door with 'Welcome Aboard' painted across it. The curtains were drawn.

Maddy knocked once, twice. "Police!"

No answer.

She exchanged a glance with Emily, then knocked again, harder.

Emily moved to the window, peering through a small gap in the curtain. "There's a mug on the table. I can just about see that it's nearly full. But I don't know, something feels off."

Maddy reached for the handle. It turned easily, the door wasn't latched properly. She stepped back and looked at her colleague. "I guess we're going in."

Inside, the air was still. Too still. As though the house itself had been holding its breath. The front room was neat, everything in place: knitted blanket folded over the back of a chair, slippers beside the sofa, a mug almost full of tea cooling on a coaster.

Emily scanned the space. "Maddy..."

Maddy moved forward, calling, "Tessa?" Her voice sounded too loud amidst the silence.

She pushed open the bedroom door and stopped. Tessa North lay fully clothed on the bed, arms by her sides, as though she'd simply decided to lie down and never got up again. Eyes closed. Still. Peaceful in a way that didn't feel right at all.

Emily stepped beside her, instinct kicking in. She checked for a pulse, breath, any sign of life. Then she met Maddy's eyes and shook her head.

Maddy's voice was steady, though her chest felt hollow. "Call it in."

This was happening too much.

The detective constable stepped back into the hallway and got on her phone, giving the address, and requesting immediate backup and a duty doctor. Maddy remained in the bedroom, her eyes tracing the edges of the scene trying to see if anything stood out. Anything at all. Even the smallest curl of a carpet could be a major clue.

The bed, beneath Tessa's lifeless body was neatly made. No sign of struggle and no overturned furniture. Her shoes sat by the wardrobe. A single photo frame rested on the bedside table, Tessa and another woman, maybe her sister, standing on a beach somewhere. Both smiling. both alive and seemingly happy.

Maddy crouched slightly, scanning the room without touching anything. There was something clinical in the air. Something faint, antiseptic.

Emily returned. "Units on the way," she informed her. "Aiming for less than ten minutes across the moors."

Maddy nodded and walked, or more like tiptoed, back through the house to the sitting room.

"This wasn't natural," she breathed, looking at the remote control resting atop the TV guide. "There's no mess. No panic. Just...calm. If it's Daniel, he staged this. It has to be him. I mean, what are the odds?"

"I hear you," her colleague responded. "But I don't know. If he's this prolific, would he really be careless enough to leave a perfectly clean scene? Wouldn't he at least try and make it look like she might have fallen or had a heart attack? Everything about this is just off."

It certainly gave them food for thought and within minutes, those same thoughts were interrupted by the sound of boots on cobbles. Two uniformed officers arrived, PC Browning and a new face, PC Lyle, both young, both wide-eyed. Maddy stepped out to meet them.

"Bedroom. No obvious cause of death. Don't touch anything," she said. "Secure the area. Keep any locals back and wait for the coroner to arrive." She looked past them at the small crowd that had started to gather.

Browning hesitated, brow furrowed. "Sorry, Sergeant, are you...?"

Emily stepped forward. "She's not here officially. But she's here. Got it?"

He nodded quickly. "Got it."

They moved to tape off the narrow yard entrance as Maddy circled the cottage again. She noted everything, dust undisturbed on the windowsills, no signs of forced entry, and outside, a single set of fresh footprints through the garden path. Larger than Tessa's.

A low murmur of radio chatter drifted from the uniforms. Maddy turned her eyes back to the bedroom window, to the still figure within. No broken glass. No pill bottles. No syringes. Nothing to explain why a healthy woman in her thirties was suddenly dead.

Instead of the coroner, the local duty doctor arrived...probably because he was the closest emergency doctor available, Maddy guessed. The doctor was a middle-aged man with deep creases around his eyes and a wind-reddened nose. He exchanged a few clipped words with the constables, then nodded at Maddy as she joined him at the front door where they both put on their shoe covers.

"I understand you were first on scene?" he asked raising an eyebrow as he spoke.

She nodded, allowing him inside first. "We were following up a concern for welfare."

He nodded, moving into the bedroom with practised calm. A few minutes passed in silence, punctuated only by the sound of gloves snapping on and the occasional scribble into his notepad.

When he came back to Maddy's side, his expression was unreadable.

"No visible injuries," he explained. "No sign of trauma. Body temp puts time of death within the last eight to ten hours."

Emily stood near the door, arms folded tightly across her chest. "So, natural causes?"

The doctor hesitated. "Maybe. But I wouldn't bet on it. You'll want the post-mortem back as soon as possible."

Maddy nodded, jaw tight. "Thank you."

They both stepped outside, needing the air. There was nothing like working a scene, piecing all the parts together.

Across the lane, Maddy caught sight of a neighbour peering nervously through a lace net curtain and crossed over. The figure disappeared on approach. Perhaps she'd seen something she shouldn't have. Or heard anything.

Maddy tapped lightly on the glass, and after a moment, an elderly woman opened the door a fraction. Her wrinkled face peered out through the gap. She took one look at Maddy and stiffened.

"I'm Detective Sergeant Frost with the North Yorkshire Police," she informed her. "I'd just like to ask if you saw one of your neighbours, Miss North, yesterday at all?"

The woman paused before she nodded slowly. "Aye, yesterday afternoon. Well, she said she was feeling better. You know, she was in a terrible accident. Had to be pulled from the sea. It was a whole palava, because Shirley from down the road saw a bit of commotion when walking her dog. Then Tess said someone had checked in on her. A man. Friendly enough, quiet. Didn't catch a name."

Maddy's stomach twisted. "A man?"

The woman nodded faintly. "Oh yes. But she was smiling. Said she was on the mend."

"Did she mention the man again? The one who checked in?" Maddy asked.

"No, love. Just that he was kind. Looked professional. I thought maybe he was one of yours..."

She trailed off.

"Did Tessa mention what he looked like at all?" Maddy asked.

The woman gave a small smile. "I asked if he was a handsome young doctor, you know, teasing like. But she laughed and said no, older gentleman. Fifties, she reckoned. Professional type. Sorry I can't be of more help. I'm not able to get out much, you see? My hip's been playing up for a long while and I..."

Maddy managed a tight smile. "Thanks. No, that's really, really helpful."

The woman's expression softened a touch, the wariness behind her eyes giving way to something more tired than fearful.

"You take care of yourself, love," she said gently. "And if you need anything just ask. I mean it. You or your friend."

Maddy nodded. "We'll be in touch if we have any more questions. Thanks again."

The door clicked shut behind her, and the narrow street felt even colder than before.

She lingered on the step a moment longer, letting the unease settle like mist in her chest, before she returned to Emily.

"That's our man," she said as she came up alongside her colleague. "He was here. And now she's dead."

Back inside the cottage, the first wave of activity had settled into a rhythm. The SOCO team had arrived, quietly moving through the rooms, documenting, photographing, and lifting trace evidence. Maddy stood in the small sitting room, eyes fixed on the coffee table where Tessa's half-finished tea had long gone cold.

Emily crouched by the sideboard, flipping open a battered

notebook she'd found tucked beneath a pile of unopened post. "She kept lists. Grocery shopping. Things to ask her GP. Then...here."

She held up a page. The writing was neat, careful.

"The man from the beach called again."

Maddy's mouth went dry. "That's him. He made contact more than once."

Emily nodded, flipping the page to find a list of names, some crossed out. At the top: Daniel. Underlined.

Maddy began pacing slowly, her voice low. "She was trying to make sense of it. Maybe even tracking him. But he got to her first."

Emily glanced up. "It's the same every time. The pattern. He saves them. Watches them. And when he decides they don't measure up..."

"They die," Maddy finished.

The pieces had always been there, scattered through autopsy reports, old ambulance call-outs, whisper-thin margins in newspaper archives. But now they had shape, form. And Tessa's death confirmed it. This wasn't a coincidence. It was orchestration.

"He saved her life three weeks ago," Maddy offered. "And now she's dead. No trauma. No toxins. Just...gone."

Emily's expression was taut with frustration. "It's like he's rewriting their fate."

"No," Maddy said, her voice sharp. "He thinks that he's correcting it. He thinks they should've died. That fate messed up, and he's just putting it right." She moved to the window and looked out at the now quiet, village. "We're dealing with someone who believes he's the hand of justice. Only his version doesn't include second chances."

* * *

Outside, the sea wind had picked up again, pushing low clouds inland and fluttering the police tape now strung across the gate. Maddy stood beside Emily near the car, staring back at the cottage as uniformed officers moved around them.

Emily had her arms crossed tightly, shoulders hunched. "This is getting harder to explain away," she said after a moment.

Maddy didn't answer straight away. Her jaw was clenched, throat dry.

"It's not meant to be explained," she said eventually. "It's meant to feel ordinary. That's his trick. He makes it look like nothing happened. No violence, no mess. Just... nothing at all."

Emily glanced sideways. "But it's not nothing. It never was."

Maddy nodded slowly. The roar of the sea was distant, a low growl at the edge of everything. The village behind them was waking up, shutters creaking open, the clang of bins being dragged, the world moving on like nothing had happened.

She looked up at the cottage window. "That woman had a second chance. She survived. And he decided she shouldn't have."

Emily stepped closer. "It's personal, isn't it? For him."

"Yeah," Maddy whispered. "And now it's personal for me too."

She turned back to the car, hands in her coat pockets just as Emily's phone buzzed. The constable pulled it out and took a couple of steps away before answering it.

"DC Emily Ward... Oh! Hi!"

Maddy watched her colleague's expression darken before she glanced at over at her.

"It's your mam," she said, frowning. "She's tried ringing you. She said she couldn't get through."

Maddy's stomach dropped. *Fuck.* She held out her hand, and Emily passed the phone over without question.

"Mam?"

Claire's voice was quiet but strained. "I didn't want to panic you, love..." she explained. "But he's been here again. I...I found something in the post this morning. No envelope, just a note, tucked through the flap."

Maddy felt her breath catch. "What did it say?"

There was a pause on the line, the faint shuffle of paper.

"'You're not the only one who remembers.'"

Maddy closed her eyes. The words shot ice through her.

"He's not just following me," she whispered. "He's digging into our past. Yours. Dad's. All of it."

Chapter Nineteen

The following morning, the sky above Whitby was the colour of ash, and the early light over the rooftops bled streaks of sullen grey. Maddy parked in the furthest corner of the station car park, where the light didn't quite reach and nobody would think to check for her car. Not because she was trying to hide, but because she didn't want to have to explain anything to anyone.

She took the contractor entrance, the one used for visiting specialists, pushing the door open with her shoulder like she belonged. Down the corridor, past the ops room and past Harper's office, it was still dark. At the end of the hall was the old conference room, the one they sometimes used for press briefings or sensitive interviews. The door was cracked open.

Dr. Vishaal Patel was adjusting equipment when she walked in. He looked up, his eyebrows arching in acknowledgment, a subtle smile hinting at the corners of his lips. The table was cluttered with a laptop cable that curled across its surface. Beside it, a packet of digestive biscuits sat forgotten, their packaging slightly crinkled, revealing that they had been there for weeks, untouched.

Emily was already seated at the far end of the table, sleeves rolled up, a pen tapping absently against her notepad. Her fringe was still damp from the shower, and there were shadows under her eyes that even her concealer hadn't managed to hide.

Maddy nodded to Patel, then slipped into the chair beside Emily.

"You should still be home," Maddy said, casting a sideways glance at Emily's pale face. "You didn't sleep much. Don't pretend you did."

Emily didn't lift her gaze from the notepad. "And let you do this alone? Someone's got to make sure you don't go rogue again."

Maddy snorted softly. "You stayed because I made proper tea and didn't shove you onto the sofa."

Emily gave a faint smirk. "Yeah, well. It was better than going home to an empty flat." She paused, then added with a shrug, "Besides, someone's got to make sure you don't burn the place down."

Their words were light, but the look they shared over the table said more. The case had them both by the throat, and neither was willing to let go. Not yet.

Momentary silence settled between them apart from the hum of the laptop. Outside in the hallway, voices rose and fell. Maddy heard brief bursts of radio chatter, the scuff of boots, and tension wrapped tight around every corner.

Dr. Patel's usual calm was replaced with an intensity she hadn't seen before. Instead of using the projector or slides laid out on the table, he slid them aside and reached for a thick folder. He rifled through it quickly, eyes scanning the pages, jaw tight. Then he looked up at the two women, and the shift in the room was immediate, anticipation crackled like static.

"I found something," he said, voice clipped and low, the kind that made your stomach turn before your brain caught up.

Maddy and Emily's eyes met, an unspoken readiness tightening their features as they leaned in to hear more.

"I reanalysed the blood panels," he continued. "Particularly from Sophie Chambers and Peter Longstaff. Something's been bothering me for a while."

Maddy nodded slowly. "And?"

"Trace levels of a cardiac suppressant. Rare. Very rare. It's used in some trauma training for anaesthetists or by specialist vets during controlled sedation. Not something you'd find lying around."

Emily frowned. "So not your average over-the-counter sedative, then?"

Patel shook his head. "This stuff acts fast. Shuts down the heart without causing any trauma. And here's the kicker, it metabolises within hours. This means that by the time a normal post-mortem is carried out, it's gone. There is no trace. I only found it because I kept on repeating the tests to make sure I'd accounted for every possible thing."

"Thank God you searched," Maddy sat back, a slow horror settling over her shoulders like a frost. "So he's drugging them. After he's saved them."

"Exactly," Patel said. "It seems like he lets them think they're recovering, then he visits again and finishes what he started. And no one suspects a thing. It looks like heart failure. Or a delayed response to trauma."

Emily was already scribbling. "Is there a name for it?" she asked, her pen lifting slightly as she paused.

Dr. Patel glanced down at his notes before facing them again.

"Medetomidine," he answered. "Usually paired with something like ketamine in field use. But in isolation, in the right dose, it's deadly."

"And he knows that," Maddy muttered. "He knows exactly what he's doing."

* * *

Once Dr. Patel packed up his things and offered them a final nod goodbye, he slipped out of the room, leaving the two women in silence. They paused only long enough to gather the papers and folders he'd left for them.

"Come on," Maddy said. "Let's go back to my desk. I want to map this properly."

The walk back through the station felt different now...more focused. They passed by the main briefing room where a few uniformed officers were gathering. Harper's door was now ajar, his silhouette visible behind his frosted window. Maddy quickened her pace just enough to avoid notice.

In the open-plan office, the morning buzz had settled in. Phones trilled, keyboards clattered, and the familiar smell of instant porridge and burnt toast wafted from the kitchen.

At her desk, Maddy dropped the folders on the surface, and Emily flopped into the spare chair beside her. It was a rare pocket of calm, and both women immediately fell into their rhythm.

Maddy wiped down the whiteboard mounted on the nearby wall and began a fresh timeline. Then she listed the victims in order, Andy Pearson, Sophie Chambers, Peter Longstaff, Tessa North, each one accompanied by dates, Daniel Cross' known whereabouts, and cause of death. Or, rather, what had once been the assumed cause of death.

Emily walked over and stood by her side, arms folded, brow furrowed. "They all died at home or in hospital. Peacefully. Nothing violent."

Maddy uncapped a red marker and circled a point. "That's

the problem. Too peaceful. He waits, gives them time to think they're safe."

"But they're not." Emily grimaced.

As Maddy drew the final red line connecting Peter Longstaff's name to a care assignment logged under Daniel Cross' old paramedic roster, a voice broke through the hum of the office.

"Em?"

They both turned to see DC Ben Travers hovering awkwardly beside Emily's desk, sausage roll in one hand, take-away coffee in the other, his ID badge swinging lopsided from his lanyard. He was in his late twenties, fresh-faced with the kind of eager energy that hadn't yet been worn down by years on the job. His shirt was perpetually untucked on one side, his tie slightly askew with the eternal look of someone who'd been running between desks all day.

"DI Pearson's asking for you," he said, nodding toward the far corridor. "Needs a warrant push on the Bentley file, says it's urgent."

Emily groaned. "Because I'm the only person in the entire building with a working printer?"

Travers smirked. "Apparently, your reputation precedes you."

Maddy smirked despite how she was feeling. She had forgotten the mundane every-day ridiculousness of this place. "Or maybe he's just scared of Harper."

Emily walked over to her desk, grabbing her notepad with a theatrical sigh. "You better not redraw my lines while I'm gone."

"Wouldn't dream of it," Maddy replied.

As Emily followed Travers out, Maddy turned back to the board. The whiteboard now looked more like a crime scene in itself, lines and loops, dates and initials, a scrawl of controlled chaos. She stared at it for a long moment, letting the silence creep back in.

And then her mobile buzzed sharply against the desk, drawing her attention away from the grim list of names.

Heard from Denton you're back sniffing around town. Fancy lunch? Got a few stories the fish won't listen to!

Maddy blinked in surprise as she recognised the name. Jack Langton.

Not a name she'd thought of in years. They'd overlapped once, barely, when she was just starting out in Whitby, before she left for London. Back then he'd been all gruff-detective energy, quiet and capable, with too much on his shoulders and not enough time for small talk.

He'd left the force abruptly, something about wanting a life that didn't revolve around drunken tourists and report deadlines. She remembered thinking it odd then, a DI with years still to serve, just...giving up. Now he worked the boats. A fisherman, of all things. She vaguely remembered hearing his brother was already doing it, so he'd bought one of the smaller trawlers, set up near the harbour and took to the water like it had been calling him all along.

Her eyes drifted back to the message.

Jack Langton, huh?

She didn't remember him being particularly charming and definitely not cheeky, but this message had a certain swagger to it. And right now, the thought of stepping away from the board, from Patel's findings and from death, was almost too tempting.

She tapped out a reply:

Hi. Long time no see! Lunch sounds good. God knows I need something that isn't caffeine or crime scenes.

They met at a tucked-away café just off the harbour, not one of the touristy spots with crab-shaped menus and neon chalkboards, but a quieter place with creaky floorboards and the smell of a good fry up drifting from the kitchen. Maddy pushed the door open to find Jack already there, nursing a mug and flipping through a paper.

He looked up.

She paused.

Jack Langton had aged well. Really damn well, in fact.

Her old colleague was broader now. Tanned from the sea. He'd let his stubble grow into a beard, trimmed neat, peppered with grey. His denim shirt was rolled at the sleeves, forearms strong, roughened from rope and weather. He looked nothing like the slightly square man she remembered from years ago.

"Detective Frost," he said with a grin. "Sarge now, ey? Still better dressed than me."

She slid into the chair opposite. "Fisherman suits you."

He chuckled. "Wasn't sure if you'd come."

"Wasn't sure if you were joking."

They ordered sandwiches, thick slices of bread, layered with bacon and cheddar, and mugs of tea strong enough to stand a spoon upright. The waitress knew Jack by name and teased him about forgetting to pay his tab last week.

"Can't believe how much the town has changed?" Maddy began, her gaze wandering over the familiar streets outside. "I hardly recognise it any more."

Jack laughed softly as he stirred his coffee. "Right? The old hardware store is now a 'boutique'. Who would've thought?" He paused, looking out at the distant waves crashing against the shore. "But some things stay the same. That's why I like the sea. It's always there, just like it used to be."

Maddy nodded, her smile fading slightly. "Yeah. It feels different, though. After Dad..." her voice trailed off for a moment. She felt the hitch in her throat, but she pushed the hurt down, as always. "Anyway...I thought staying away would help me heal faster. I didn't know what else to do. Then, coming back was supposed to help me find some peace, but sometimes it feels more complicated than I expected."

"Really sorry about your old man," Jack said, his eyes searching hers as he rested a warm, roughened hand over hers. "It rocked a lot of us. But I hear you, I get it. I've had my own battles. I wake up before dawn so it's just me and that sea mist. It's peaceful out there, me, my thoughts and the gulls. But I realised something: I can't go back to the force. It was killing me, Mads, and I didn't even see it at first."

Maddy nodded. She could understand the motivation...but not the certainty. Those in the police force had a tendency of sticking to it, or coming back in some circular fashion. Maybe as private security, or a private eye, or bodyguard. She guessed something in them – in *her* – was hardwired that way. That's why she was surprised to hear such certainty coming from her old colleague.

"You really won't go back?" she said softly.

"No, I can't. I thought having a badge would give me purpose, but it took everything out of me. And it's hard when most of our old team has moved on to Hull or York. It's just not the same without them."

Maddy looked thoughtful. "I miss them too," she responded, thinking over how her return to Whitby almost felt incomplete without the familiar faces she'd joined with. They'd felt like family at one point. A few of them she'd known since school.

"I heard Sam is in York now," she added. Apparently, he's running a small unit, and I think Annie's in Hull. Oh, and I'm sure Gemma got a job there too. They really brought some life to the place, didn't they? It feels odd to think we've all scattered like that."

"Yeah," Jack replied, a faint smile touching his lips. "It's strange to think of everything we went through together."

Maddy let out a breath, surprised at how much she missed moments like this. "I'm glad you're finding your way, Jack. One thing's for certain, we all deserve that."

He smiled gently. "And what about you? What's next for you? I see you got promoted to Sergeant while down south."

With a thoughtful look, Maddy shrugged. She didn't exactly have a lot of great things to say about the Met in general, or about London in particular. The capital was a machine. It wore you down and wore you out, then spat you back where you came from.

"I don't know, honestly. I suppose I need to reconnect with the things that matter to me...and figure out what new things I can explore."

He nodded, a hint of encouragement in his eyes. "Well, let's help each other find our footing again."

They shared a moment of understanding, two old friends navigating their new realities as the café buzzed around them.

Maddy watched him over her mug. She hadn't felt calm like this in weeks.

When the bill came, he snatched it up with a wink. "Call it a welcome back. You can get the next one."

"Next one?"

"Assuming I didn't bore you to death."

She shook her head, smiling in spite of herself.

Outside, the wind carried the salt in sharp lashes. She stood for a moment, hand on the door frame, reluctant to go.

Jack leaned close, his voice lower. "If you need anything, info, names, gossip, then it's the watermen you should be asking. They know everything going on in this town, I promise you. If there's something you want to know, use me."

Their eyes met.

And for once, Maddy didn't feel alone in this.

She nodded. "I might take you up on that," she said, before turning back toward the station, heart just a little lighter.

* * *

Later that evening, the golden light outside the station began to bleed into a soft amber haze, and inside the station Emily pushed back from her chair with a groan, stretching out her spine. She blinked at the whiteboard covered in thick timeline loops of red ink, then turned to Maddy, who was still hunched over a page of Daniel Cross' employment records, eyes narrowed in scrutiny.

"Right," Emily said, trying for casual but falling short. "I'm heading off. I've done what I can on the Chambers timeline for now. I can't do too much for Travers until I get CCTV from the hotel. Honestly, I need a proper night before I lose track of what day it is."

Maddy didn't look up immediately. She made a note in the margin of a printout, then glanced over. "You walking home?"

"Yeah. Bus was late this morning, and I need the air."

Maddy studied her for a moment. "You sure? If you hang about I can drop you off. Maybe another thirty minutes. I just need to finish off going through this..."

Emily hesitated before a smile crept across her face. "Positive. I'm shattered and all I want to do is jump in the bath and soak. I'll be fine. I'll text you when I'm in, I know the drill."

"Alright," Maddy said, but her eyes lingered too long. "You've got your alarm thingy?"

Emily patted her coat pocket. "Never without it."

Maddy nodded. "Still. Keep your eyes up. And don't walk the alleys near the flats. Go the long way if you have to."

Emily gave a faint smile, touched with weariness. "I will. Are you going to be alright here?"

"I've got company," Maddy said, gesturing to the mess of files with a tired smile. "Daniel's history is riveting."

Emily snorted. Any attempt at humour, it seemed, was welcome with what they were dealing with. "Night, Sarge."

"Night, Em. Message me, yeah?"

"Promise."

Emily gathered her belongings and made her way towards the main corridor, saying a couple of goodbyes to the skeleton crew on her way out. The silence that followed was oddly heavy.

Maddy exhaled, the fluorescent strobe lights casting a harsh pool of light over the documents, and the hum of voices on the street outside was the only sound keeping her company. She was cross-referencing the old patient discharge sheets Dr. Patel had forwarded with the handwritten reports left by her father when her phone buzzed, vibrating sharply against the desk. Looking down, she saw Emily's name on her screen. Maddy's brow furrowed. She answered instantly.

"I'm fine."

It was the first thing Emily said, which told her exactly the opposite.

"What the hell happened?" she asked sharply.

The constable's voice was shaky. "Someone was waiting outside my flat. I...I didn't see them, just got shoved. Hard. And hit the wall. Don't worry, nothing's broken, but they just ran off."

Maddy was already grabbing her coat. Her keys jangled in her hand. "Did they say anything?"

"One thing," Emily said quietly. "They said: Leave it.'"

Maddy's chest burned as she stood abruptly, nearly sending

her chair screeching back across the floor. "You're off the case. No arguments."

Emily's voice caught as she answered, still slightly shaken. "Mads, I can still help..."

"No," Maddy snapped, then immediately softened as the word hung heavy between them. "No. You're hurt, you're scared, and he knows where you live. This isn't up for discussion."

On the other end of the line, Emily was silent for a moment, save for a shaky exhale. "You'd do the same for me," she said finally. "Don't pretend you wouldn't."

Maddy clenched her jaw, pacing now, her fingers curled tight around the phone. "I have done the same for you. But this is different. It's not some nameless threat any more. It's here. In Whitby. In your street."

Emily's voice was steadier now, but the underlying fear was still there. "He didn't hurt me, not properly. He just made a point. He's watching us."

"That's exactly why you're done," Maddy said, quieter now, almost pleading. "I need to know you're safe, Em. I can't do this if I'm constantly waiting for my phone to ring again with that call. Let me do this. Let me take it from here."

A moment passed. Then, reluctantly, Emily responded. "Okay... Fine. But only for now. You call me if anything shifts, and Maddy... don't shut me out completely."

Maddy swallowed the lump in her throat. "Wouldn't dream of it. Give me a couple of minutes and I'll come by."

The detective constable gave a strained laugh.

"Don't," she responded, but Maddy could hear that Emily was shaken. Resigned. "Honestly I'm okay. Really, we just...we just can't let him win."

* * *

Her mother's cottage was quiet when Maddy let herself in. Her mother was still awake, sat in her chair with a cross-stitch project untouched in her lap.

"You're late, Madeline," she said, eyes fixed on her daughter. "I was worried so I waited up. What with everything that's been going on lately."

Maddy slumped into the opposite chair, weariness threatening to overcome her. "Emily was aggressively approached outside her flat."

'Aggressively approached' Maddy thought. That was the kind of phrase she'd write down on an incident report. *What it means is some douche tried to take a swipe at her.* Maddy was fuming and angry, and she didn't like her mother seeing her like this.

Claire's expression tightened. "God, is she alright? Did she get hurt?" There was a plate with some biscuits on her coffee table and she gestured to them.

Maddy reached forward and took one. "She's fine," she answered. "Shaken. But she's still alive and not hurt."

Claire was quiet for a long moment, looking down at the cross-stitch pattern lying limp in her lap. "This man doesn't care about rules, Maddy. He's not just clever, he's cruel. Cold. And the worst part is, he's patient. That's the kind of danger that creeps in when no one's looking."

Maddy swallowed hard. "I keep telling my boss, but it's like shouting into the wind. He says we don't have enough concrete evidence and can't act on hunches or patterns. But it's more than that. I think he's afraid. Afraid of what it means if I'm right."

Her Mam looked up then, her eyes dark and full of something unspoken. "Of course he is. Because if you're right, it means there's a killer walking among us and the system didn't see it. Or worse, ignored it."

Maddy leaned forward, elbows on her knees. "He won't back me. Not unless I put a body on his desk with the paramedic's name carved into it."

There was a tremble in Claire's voice now. "It wasn't like this when your father was working. I mean, we had problems, sure. But not like this, not this weight. God, I miss him so much, Mads. Every moment in every day."

Maddy inhaled deeply, trying and failing to suppress any personal thoughts of her father. She'd promised herself that any memories of him would be purely professional, but it was impossible. Her father was everywhere back here, in this home and in this town. His favourite mug still in the back of the cupboard, his collection of vinyl in the display cabinet. Even his toothbrush was lying in the drawer under the bathroom sink. The cottage was loaded with his echo in every fibre and for a split second, it felt suffocating.

Claire got up, punctuating the silence as she shuffled over to Maddy and pulled her into her arms.

"You don't always have to be this strong detective," she pointed out. "You lost your father. You're allowed to grieve. You're allowed to feel something, and I hate that this case is stirring it all up again."

"I miss him too," Maddy sniffed quietly. "I'm so angry that he left us, but I fucking miss him. Damnit!" She pulled away and wiped at her face, embarrassed slightly that she'd fallen back on her promise to herself. She's promised herself that she'd be strong for her Mam. That coming back to Whitby was as much about supporting her as it was getting away from the Met.

"He'd be proud of you, Mads," Claire said, watching her before she settled herself back onto her chair. "He always was. Even when you left to fight crime with the southerners, he couldn't have been prouder."

Maddy nodded, blinking back any emotion that threatened to push its way forward.

"That's why I have to see this though," she responded. "And I think this might all be connected somehow. I just need more time."

Claire reached across and took her daughter's hand. "Then you be smart, darling. Be careful. And don't do it alone. I already lost one of you, and I can't lose another."

* * *

Upstairs, in her bedroom, Maddy sat at the foot of her bed. She'd brought a few of her dad's old notebooks up with her. She flipped through one of them, its pages smudged and stained. She could almost imagine him sat there going through it all the clues and piecing every tiny clue together. Had the case given him sleepless nights too? Had he been on the verge of finding out something?

As she flipped through the pages near the back, something caught her eye. Tucked between a crumpled report and a folded napkin serving as a makeshift bookmark was a document. Curious, she pulled it free and examined it closely. It was a summary file, unadorned by official crests or classification stamps. Instead, a single handwritten note sprawled across the top:

PERSONAL – NOT CLEARED.

The weight of those words sent a chill down her spine, hinting at secrets buried beneath the surface. Her heart thumped. She unfolded the paper, the sound slicing through the silence. The report detailed a near-fatal car crash on a lonely North Yorkshire lane. The driver had survived.

Then, halfway down the page, a name caught her eye: Sarah Cross.

Maddy froze. A chill ran down her spine. She had no idea who Sarah was, but something about the name twisted in her gut, a sense of dread rising within her.

She stared at the letters, her heart pounding and without thinking, she grabbed a pen and circled the name, and then did it again.

Chapter Twenty

The kettle had just started to whistle when Claire's voice sliced through the sound of another day starting.

"Madeline, you've not even touched that toast."

Maddy sat at the kitchen table, elbow propped on the surface, fingers curling into her hair. Her eyes were fixed on the aged notebook in front of her. The name scrawled in faded ink at the top of the page, Sarah Cross, burned into her mind like a brand. Her dad's handwriting, too neat to belong to a man who'd lived his entire life by the sea, framed it with underlines and tiny annotations. It was tagged PERSONAL – NOT CLEARED.

"Thanks Mam, but I'm not hungry," she muttered, eyes still glued to the file. "And, wait, did you just call me Madeline?"

Her mother clattered a mug down beside her with more force than necessary. "You say that every morning, and yes, you're never too old for a stern 'full name'!"

Maddy smirked despite herself, finally glancing up. Her mother was bustling about the little kitchen as though she was hosting the Queen. Still in her dressing gown, hair shoved up with a scrunchie, and slippers that had seen better years, she looked like half the middle-aged mothers in Whitby. Comfortable and familiar, but the creases at the corners of her eyes, the way her lips pressed tightly together, those were new.

Her father's death had taken its toll on her and that was part of the reason Maddy felt she had to come back. Life felt too short now. She'd been keen to rent a flat further towards the edge of town but her mother had insisted she move back into her childhood home for a bit to stick together. It did absolutely nothing for her personal life, but they were all each other had and she couldn't imagine losing another parent. Not yet.

Claire stopped moving and looked back at her, glancing down at the papers she had out on the table. "What's this one then? Another name? Same case?"

Maddy hesitated. Her hand hovered over the page before she pushed it gently towards her mam.

"Sarah Cross."

Claire peered down, adjusting her glasses. "Cross? Hmmm...same last name. Any relation to the paramedic?"

Maddy ran a hand through her hair.

"Honestly? I don't know yet," she answered. "But the name was in one of Dad's old notes. Just her name, no rank, no job title, no info. Just...there."

Claire reached for the kettle and poured hot water into the waiting mugs. Steam rose between them.

"I mean, it could just be coincidence," she offered. "Lots of people have the same name, right?" Silence hung between them before she continued. "I'm guessing you didn't sleep last night?"

Maddy sighed and rested back in her chair.

"Not much," she admitted.

"I can tell," her mam said softly. "You've got that haunted look. The same one you had when you were twelve and swore blind you hadn't broken the greenhouse window."

"That was you," Maddy said dryly with a wry smile. "I just covered for you."

Claire raised her mug in salute. "Good daughter."

They sat in silence for a moment, the only sound the gentle ticking of the clock on the wall and the occasional seagull call from outside.

"You know," Claire said breaking the silence, "just once, I'd like you to look at a name and not see death waiting on the other side."

Maddy stared at the file again. "Me too. But if she's alive, I need to find her. And I need to understand why dad thought she was relevant enough to write down."

Claire moved to the table, setting her tea down and reaching across to take Maddy's hand. "Just promise me you're not doing this to chase ghosts. Your dad wouldn't want you tearing yourself apart. Not like this."

Maddy met her mother's gaze. "I don't know what he'd want anymore, Mam. But I know I need to see this through."

Claire squeezed her hand. "Then you do it. But don't lose yourself in the process."

The morning light through the window cast gold across the kitchen table, catching on the worn edge of the file. Maddy closed it with a decisive snap.

"I'll try not to."

The station was quieter than usual when Maddy walked in, the kind of lull that came after a storm, but before anyone knew whether to relax or brace for round two. She passed the incident board on the main wall, with crossed names and pinned reports glared back at her.

Emily was already in the back office, scrolling through the local press archive and open-source web data on the desktop. A faint purple bruise marked her wrist where someone had grabbed her the night before, barely visible beneath her pushed-up sleeve. She caught Maddy looking and tugged the fabric down. A stack of FOI requests sat beside her, half-filled out, each one a long shot to access what they really needed.

"You're supposed to be resting," Maddy whispered, tossing her coat over the back of a chair. They'd decided the fewer people knew about them still chasing the paramedic the better.

Emily glanced up, brow raised. "Resting's for civilians, remember. You find anything?"

Maddy joined her, logging into her own computer. She noticed Emily glance towards the window for the third time since she'd arrived. "You doing alright?"

"Fine," Emily said automatically, then caught Maddy's look. She touched the faint bruise on her wrist briefly. "Harper made me see the force counsellor before he'd sign me back to full duty. Took a bit of convincing that I was ready."

"And are you?"

"I changed my route to work. Park in view of cameras now. Harper's got patrols doing extra passes by my flat." Emily's jaw set. "I'm being careful, but I'm not hiding. He doesn't get to scare me off this case."

Maddy studied her partner for a moment, then nodded. "Good. But you tell me if that changes."

"Deal."

"Thank you," she answered as she continued setting up her computer. "And, to answer your question, all I found was a name. Sarah Cross. She came up in one of my dad's old files. No context, no details. But I've got a hunch."

"That's dangerous," Emily smirked. "I've seen what your hunches lead to."

"Yeah," Maddy muttered, "so have I."

They fell into a rhythm of typing, searching, and cross-checking. Coffee grew cold beside them. Outside, the light shifted across the narrow windows, casting long shadows over evidence boards and filing cabinets.

Then Emily made a small noise, sharp and focused. "Found something. Accident report from almost ten years ago. Sarah Denton-Cross. Twenty-eight at the time. Head-on collision outside Sleights. She died on the way to the hospital."

Maddy leaned over her shoulder. "Who was the paramedic on scene?"

Emily clicked and scrolled. "Daniel Cross."

The words hung in the air like smoke.

Maddy straightened, swallowing the sudden tightness in her throat. "So she wasn't saved. Perhaps she was the one he couldn't rescue."

Emily nodded slowly. "And what if now...he doesn't think anyone else deserves to be."

Maddy stared at the screen, heart racing as some of the pieces clicked together. Sarah Denton-Cross. Maybe Daniel's wife or even his sister?

Maddy turned to the board, her hand shaking as she picked up the marker. One by one, she circled the victims again. Then drew a single line through the centre.

Sarah Denton-Cross.

Not the first victim.

The first echo.

Maddy's phone buzzed insistently in her pocket as she pulled up her jacket collar against the brisk sea breeze that had made its way inland from the coast. The chill in the air was a shock after the stifling warmth of the station, and she stepped outside for a moment, looking for clarity among the chaos. Her fingers fumbled, but she answered the call just before it rang off.

"DS Frost."

"Maddy, it's Dr. Patel."

She braced herself. "Tell me you've found something we can use."

"I've been re-analysing the toxicology data on Sophie Chambers and Tessa North using a forensic pharmacologist we occasionally work with at Hull Royal. I thought you should hear this directly."

Maddy's breath caught. "Go on."

"There is indeed a compound, same one we flagged before, but I've got more context now. It's not just a cardiac suppressant. It's something typically used in certain anaesthetic trials, experimental stuff. Has to be administered in micro-doses and metabolises within hours. Not part of the usual NHS medical inventory. It's tightly restricted."

"How the hell would he get his hands on that?"

"That's the point. This isn't being lifted from the supply cupboard of a GP surgery. This is either black market or leftover from a very specific clinical trial."

"Is there a way to trace it?"

"Not easily. There are no batch markers left in the victims. It's too clean. But if we had an idea of which hospitals the guy worked in during the past decade, we might be able to cross-check against any study involvement or supply mismanagement."

Maddy turned away from the wind, phone pressed tightly to her ear. "Even if I did, I can't just go nosing through NHS records without a judge and ten layers of red tape."

"I know. But there's something else." Patel hesitated, then continued. "I looked again at the adrenaline profiles. These weren't natural panic responses. They were primed. The victims weren't just afraid. Their nervous systems were hijacked. Whoever did this knew exactly how to create the perfect cocktail of chemical terror."

Maddy closed her eyes. "He was playing god."

"Worse," Patel replied. "He was re-enacting something. That sort of precision, that repeatability, it's not a random thrill. It's ritual."

Confirmation of what she had already known did not come with any sense of relief, just bitterness. Daniel Cross was displaying all the hallmarks of criminal, obsessive psychopathy. Ritualised behavior. Tight control of victim, scene, and murder.

She ended the call in silence and stood for a moment in the thin grey light. Her reflection shimmered faintly in the glass of the car window. Somewhere out there, Daniel Cross was still operating. Still controlling. Still choosing.

And now she had a brand new thread to pull. Don't mess this up.

* * *

Maddy sat alone in the staff room, nursing a mug of tea that had long since gone cold. The station's hum felt distant now, the occasional murmur of voices, the shuffle of paperwork, and the clatter of someone's keyboard beyond the half-closed door. She stared at the table's worn surface, fingers idly tracing a knot in the wood. The air smelt faintly of cheap coffee and disinfectant, comforting in its familiarity.

The door creaked open and Emily appeared, shrugging off her jacket, hair slightly windswept from being outside. She dropped into the chair opposite Maddy, watching her for a beat before speaking.

"You've been at this since first light. Why don't you knock off for a bit?"

Maddy shook her head. "And do what? Go home and stare at the ceiling?"

Before Emily could answer, Maddy's phone buzzed against the table. She glanced down, it was Jack Langton. The unexpected sight of his name softened something her just for a second.

She unlocked the screen, reading the message.

"Hey you. Hope today's not been a total nightmare. Fancy grabbing that drink soon? Could use a distraction."

Emily peered at the screen. "Ah, the hunky fisherman-slash-ex-copper. That's a distraction worth taking."

Maddy rolled her eyes, but her lips twitched at the corners. "Maybe."

Before she could tap out a reply, the door opened again and one of the younger detectives, PC Dan Riley, poked his head in. He was barely out of probation, all sharp cheekbones and nervous energy.

"Sorry to interrupt, Emily, DI Harper's looking for you about that missing woman. Wants your take on the patterns."

Emily groaned good-naturedly, standing. "Can't say no to that, can I?"

She gave Maddy's shoulder a squeeze as she passed. "Don't sit in here all day."

Maddy watched her go, the room settling into quiet again. She exhaled slowly, picking up her phone, but instead of replying to Jack, her thumb hesitated, then moved to her browser.

Sarah Denton-Cross.

She typed the name in, the letters stark against the white screen. The search results trickled in. An obituary from years ago, short, formal, with a black-and-white photo that made Maddy's stomach knot. A fundraiser page from back then, friends trying to cover funeral costs, filled with comments about how kind and full of life Sarah had been. A staff memorial notice from the ambulance trust, offering condolences to her 'loving and devoted' husband...Daniel Cross. *Bingo*!

Maddy clicked through, absorbing every detail, her pulse

steady but heavy in her ears. The woman in the photo had that soft, open smile, the same one she'd seen echoes of in the victims. Dark hair, expressive brows, warm eyes that seemed to look straight through the camera.

Her throat felt tight. It wasn't coincidence. He'd been chasing her all along. Recreating her.

Maddy sat back, the hum of the station returning to her ears. Behind her, beyond the staff room door, the world carried on. But in that moment, all she could see were those faces, the ones he'd chosen. The ones who, in some way must have, reminded him of her.

Chapter Twenty-One

Maddy lingered by the staff room door for a moment, thumb hovering over her phone screen. The photos, the obituary, the GoFundMe, they all churned in her head like storm waves against the pier. She couldn't just sit on this. Emily had to see it too.

The office beyond buzzed with subdued energy: phones ringing, keys clacking, muted conversations that blurred together. Emily was across the room, bent over a file with that same intense frown she got when she was trying to will the pieces of a puzzle into place.

Maddy crossed to her, quiet but purposeful. "Em?"

Emily glanced up, immediately clocking the look on Maddy's face. "What's happened?"

"Come here." Maddy gestured her over to the quietest corner she could find, near the side exit where the vending machine hummed uselessly.

When they stopped, Maddy handed over her phone. "I found her. The one from Dad's file. Sarah Denton-Cross."

Emily scrolled through the screen, absorbing the details, the fundraiser comments, the obituary, the old black-and-white photo. Her expression shifted from curious to grim. "Bloody hell."

"Look at her." Maddy tapped the image gently. "Tell me she doesn't look like them. Sophie. Tessa. All of them."

Emily's throat worked as she swallowed. "Yeah. I see it."

"He's been chasing her, Em. Or...what she represented. The funeral fund I found...Daniel Cross was listed as her husband. This wasn't just about a random victim. She was his wife. He lost her that day, and I think Daniel decided no one else should get what she didn't...a second chance."

Emily handed the phone back, eyes sharp now. "So what's next?"

Before Maddy could answer, the phone on her desk rang. One of the uniformed constables waved her over. "Harper wants a word in his office."

Maddy exchanged a glance with Emily. "Great," she muttered, pocketing her phone. She made her way down the corridor and knocked before pushing the door open.

Harper sat behind his desk, the lines around his eyes deeper than usual. He gestured to the chair opposite. "Sit down, Frost."

She did, wary. "Sir?"

Harper rubbed a hand over his face, looking for a moment less like her boss and more like a tired man trying to keep all the pieces together. "I wanted to say, I was hard on you before. Too hard. This case is getting to all of us."

Maddy blinked, surprised. "Thank you. I know you're just trying to keep things from spiralling."

He nodded, gaze steady. "What are you working on now?"

Maddy hesitated. "Following threads. I don't want to bring you half a theory. When I've got something solid, you'll be the first to know."

Harper glowered for a moment, because Maddy had just admitted to ignoring his express orders. That was insubordination. That was enough for a suspension, or at least an official investigation.

But did Harper want police ombudsmen sniffing around his station? Maddy considered. Clearly not, as he studied her for a long moment, then gave a small nod. "All right. But be careful. I'm trusting you not to go too far with this. Don't cut corners, don't leave me in the dark. I need to know what you're doing, when you're doing it. We can't afford another mess."

"I will." She stood, relief mingling with tension. "Thanks, sir," she said, and she meant it.

* * *

It was late by the time Maddy let herself into the house. The familiar creak of the floorboards under her boots was oddly comforting, grounding her after the day's chaos. The living room was dark except for the glow of a lamp her mam must have left on for her.

Claire's voice drifted from the kitchen. "That you, love?"

"Yeah, Mam, it's me." Maddy hung her coat, rubbing at her face with both hands before stepping through.

Her mam was at the table, nursing a mug of tea, her hair tied back in a loose knot. She looked up, concern etching deep lines around her eyes. "You look done in."

"I am," Maddy admitted, sinking into the chair opposite. She hesitated, then added, "I found something today. Something big. But it's...a lot."

Claire reached across, resting a warm hand over hers. "Tell me, pet."

Maddy drew in a breath, steadying herself before she spoke. "It's Sarah Cross. You know, the name from Dad's file. I found her obituary, Mam, and it turns out she died in a car accident.

She died at the scene and she's his wife. She was married to Daniel Cross."

Her mam's brows drew together, her thumb gently rubbing circles over Maddy's knuckles. "God! And you think this is where it all started for him?"

Maddy nodded, her voice low, the words almost sticking in her throat. "Yeah. I think losing her broke something in him. Like, if he couldn't save Sarah, no one else deserved to be saved either. Every victim...Sophie, Tessa, they all look like her, Mam. Like he's trying to erase second chances, because she never got hers."

Claire's eyes misted, and she gripped Maddy's hand tightly. "God...that's heartbreaking. And terrifying that instead of managing his grief, he used it to inflict pain on others."

Maddy swallowed hard, her throat tight. "It is. But it's also something I can use. If I can prove it and tie it all together, maybe we can finally stop him."

Claire nodded, fierce beneath the worry in her gaze. "You will. I know you will. Just promise me you'll be careful. Promise me you'll come home safe and that when all of this gets too...much that'll you hand the information over and step away."

"I promise, Mam," Maddy said, though the knot in her chest told her how hard keeping that promise would be.

Her mam squeezed her hand. "You'll get him, love. You'll see it through."

Maddy nodded, but her heart still felt heavier than ever.

Chapter Twenty-Two

The noise inside Whitby Police Station slammed into Maddy like a wave the moment she stepped through the front doors. Phones were ringing, voices shouting in a rising din that carried through the building. It wasn't just background bustle any more—it was chaos. The kind that threatened to spill into panic.

The article, Maddy realised at once.

The article had been live for a few days now, and the fallout was still unfolding. They'd been fielding calls and emails nonstop since the headline dropped, each one another flicker of possibility—another person thinking they'd spotted a pattern, another claim of a near-death experience tied to a kind-eyed paramedic who didn't quite seem right. Most had been false alarms, harmless nonsense from armchair detectives or the over-imaginative. But today felt different. The volume of calls had risen sharply. And more than that, the tone had shifted. The voices on the other end weren't just speculative—they were scared.

Maddy shrugged out of her coat, her shoulders tight with a mix of anticipation and dread. She crossed the station floor towards her desk, dodging a trailing extension cord and the scent of burnt toast from someone's long-forgotten breakfast. Emily was already on the phone, headset crooked, one hand tapping notes onto a pad while her other clicked frantically through browser tabs.

"Yeah, we're looking into that, sir—no, I understand—but if you could just give me the details of where it happened—"

Harper's voice bellowed from the corridor off the main hub, sharp and irritable as he corralled two probationers who looked like they were about to bolt.

The incident board had ballooned since the article went live. What had once been a modest collection of names and photos now looked like a conspiracy theorist's corkboard—red thread linking faces, post-it notes scrawled in messy shorthand, arrows pointing toward known addresses and unanswered questions. Still, nothing concrete. Just a map of maybes. Maddy stood there for a second longer, eyes flitting over each connection, each missing piece.

Then a voice behind her snapped.

"Frost. My office. Now."

She turned to see Harper already halfway down the corridor, the tilt of his shoulders unreadable. She followed.

The blinds were half-drawn inside the superior's, throwing striped shadows across the grey carpet. He wasn't seated. Instead, he stood by the window, hands shoved in his trouser pockets, staring out at the drizzle that pattered the courtyard paving stones.

He turned then, his jaw tight. "The bloody floodgates have opened, Maddy! The article's out. The town's buzzing. We've had more information come in over the past three days than we did in the last month. And guess whose name is being whispered on every street corner?"

"I didn't name him," she reinforced.

"You didn't have to. You made him visible." He paced toward his desk, then back again. "So now you're riding the storm you stirred, but you're not freelancing any more, Frost. No more leaks. No more secrets. If you so much as hint to the press again, I'll have your lanyard and your warrant card on this desk."

"I hear you."

A pause. Then Harper nodded once, almost like he hated himself for doing it. "Good. Now get out there and make all this bloody noise mean something."

Maddy barely made it back to her desk before Detective Constable Dan Riley flagged her down, juggling two phones and a clipboard with a kind of frantic grace only he could pull off.

"Sarge! Got one."

She blinked. "One what? If it's another bloke claiming his dog can sniff out killers, I'm not biting."

He thrust a printed form toward her. "Woman rang in and said she only just read the article. Thinks she met the man you're looking for about ten years ago."

Maddy's eyes skimmed the page. Margaret Leighton. Daughter, Elena, car crash. Attentive paramedic. Wanted to speak to someone senior.

"Is she here now?"

"Interview Room Two. Just this minute walked in."

Emily reappeared like a spectre bearing caffeine, handing her a takeaway coffee without a word. Maddy nodded toward the hallway.

"Come on. Let's see what she's got."

Margaret Leighton looked like she'd stepped straight out of a 1950s etiquette book, with her cardigan neatly buttoned, her hair pinned back, and handbag perched on the table as though afraid of germs. But her expression was taut, and her knuckles were white where they clutched each other.

"Mrs Leighton," Maddy said, softening her tone. "I'm Detective Sergeant Frost, this is Detective Constable Ward. Thanks for coming in."

Margaret nodded stiffly. "I don't know if it's useful, but after I read that article, I couldn't stop thinking about it."

"Take your time," Emily said, opening her notebook.

"My daughter, Elena was in a crash. Ten years ago, give or take, just outside Ruswarp. She was unconscious for four days. I didn't leave the hospital once."

Maddy nodded slowly. "Go on."

"There was a paramedic who came to check in on her after his shift. But he didn't just pop in...he sat for a while. On one of the days a nurse told me it was for a few hours. I thought it was weird then, creepy!"

Emily glanced at Maddy.

"I know it was all relatively strange," Maddy pressed, "but was there anything that stood out to you as being a bit more unusual?"

The older woman thought for a moment and nodded slowly.

"Well," she began, "I did think it tad odd that he got a bit firm on the phone with one of the nurses for not calling him back to update him on Elena's condition. And..." Margaret's voice lowered. "Once, I'd stepped out of her hospital room to call my husband and when I came back, he was hovering by the window and said to me, 'She suits the name Sarah.'"

The silence in the room thickened.

"I thought it was odd because I have a sister called Sarah so I thought maybe he knew her, or he was just confused."

"But it stayed with you," Maddy added.

Margaret nodded. "And when I saw that article..."

Emily murmured, "He's been doing this longer than we thought."

Maddy, quieter still, replied, "He's been looking for her everywhere."

* * *

Back at their desks, Emily scoured the digital archives while Maddy paced behind her.

"There it is!" She announced. "Here's the report! Paramedic attending the scene: Daniel Cross."

They both stared at the screen. Elena's face gazed back—dark hair, kind eyes, same soft features that echoed through every victim.

"He wasn't killing then," Emily said.

"No," Maddy replied. "He was watching, waiting. Testing the waters. Maybe everything else hadn't occurred to him yet"

She stepped back, arms folded tightly across her chest.

Emily pulled up a second tab. "Let's show Harper."

* * *

Detective Inspector Harper flicked through the printouts, each page a brick added to the growing wall.

"He called the woman's daughter Sarah and sat by her bed," Maddy said. "It's not just odd. It's calculated."

"Not enough to charge him," Harper muttered.

"No," Emily said, "but enough to prove he's been escalating. There's a pattern now."

He rubbed his jaw and sighed. "Fine. Quiet digging. Nothing public. I mean it, Frost."

Maddy gave him a crisp nod in return. "Understood."

* * *

Later, the harbour air nipped at Maddy's face as she strolled along the seawall, the rhythmic sound of waves crashing against the stones creating a familiar backdrop. The salt in the air was brisk, invigorating, and yet it couldn't fully lift her spirits. Jack was there, sitting casually on the railing, his rugged silhouette framed by the fading light of day. In one hand, he held a bag of steaming chips, the aroma drifting toward her like a welcome invitation.

"You look like someone kicked your dog," he remarked with a lopsided grin, offering her one.

Maddy smirked, accepting one as she joined him on the railing. "Rough day," she admitted, the weight of her week settling in her chest.

"You mean rough week," he corrected, his blue eyes sparkling with a hint of mischief. As they walked side by side, the silence stretched comfortably between them, broken only by the rhythmic lapping of the waves against the stones below.

Jack nudged her lightly with his shoulder, his casual demeanour quietly inviting her to open up. "You've got that look," he noted, his tone shifting slightly to something more earnest.

"What look?" she asked, arching an eyebrow as they continued along the seawall.

"The one that says you're already thinking three steps ahead while forgetting to breathe." He shot her a knowing smile, one that seemed to bypass any pretence and dive straight to the heart of the matter.

With a huff of laughter, Maddy shook her head. "Is it really that obvious?"

"Only to someone who sees it in the mirror," he replied, his gaze steady and warm. Behind Jack's playful exterior, there was an understanding in his eyes that made her feel both seen and safe.

They found a bench and settled onto it, sharing chips in comfortable silence. Her mind wandered onto work, the stress of preventing more deaths, and the pressure of expectations to nail Daniel Cross that loomed larger every day. Jack had once walked that path with her during their time in the police force, and she couldn't help but feel a tug of nostalgia for the life they had once shared.

"Things have been...complicated at work," she confessed, surprising even herself with the words. It felt strangely freeing to let him in, to acknowledge the chaos that had begun to overshadow her days. "Sometimes I don't know how I'm going to make it through."

Jack listened attentively, his expression shifting to one of concern. "You know, it's okay to take a step back. I left the force because I needed a change of pace. Fishing hasn't exactly been a walk in the park, but it's helped me find perspective. Sometimes you need to strip everything back to figure out what really matters."

Maddy glanced at him, taking in the lines of his rugged face, the way the fading sunlight cast warm highlights in his hair. "I envy how grounded you are, Jack. You seem to have found your rhythm out here."

His smile softened, and there was an intensity in his gaze that made her heart race just a little faster. "It's not always easy, but it's worthwhile. You don't have to carry everything alone, you know."

As they sat together, sharing chips while the sun dipped low over the horizon, Maddy felt an unspoken understanding beginning to weave itself between them. It lingered in the air around them, wrapped in the sound of the sea and the warmth of shared silence, and it was the perfect momentary distraction that she needed from the case. Just enough to reset her overwhelmed mind.

When Maddy got home, the living room was dim, telly flickering softly in the corner with the sound of some awful re-run celebrity reality show. Her mam had fallen asleep on the sofa, her chin resting on her chest, glasses askew and one slipper half-hanging off her foot. Maddy paused in the doorway, taking in the peaceful sight before gently switching off the TV and pulling the throw up over her mother's shoulders. Her movements were slow, careful, as if noise might wake the fragile quiet of the moment.

Maddy paused, really looking at her mother for the first time in weeks. Claire seemed smaller somehow, as though grief had hollowed her out from the inside. The lines around her eyes had deepened, her cheeks more drawn than Maddy remembered. Even in sleep, there was a tightness to her expression that hadn't been there before. A tension that never quite left, even in rest.

The cross-stitch hoop sat abandoned on the side table, its pattern half-finished. Her parents used to work on projects together in the evenings. Her father restoring old furniture in the shed whilst her mam stitched by the fire, their quiet companionship filling the room. Now the shed sat locked and unused, tools gathering dust, and Claire's cross-stitch lay neglected more often than not. The silence in the house had changed. It wasn't peaceful anymore. It was empty.

She glanced down to see one of her dad's old photo albums lying open on the coffee table, its leather spine worn from years of use. Curiosity tugged at her. She knelt and pulled it onto her lap, her fingers tracing the edge of the pages. Each photograph was like a whisper from the past. Him in his RNLI gear back when he used to volunteer, grinning by a lifeboat; another, with his arm slung around a fellow crew member, the salt wind turning his fringe wild.

As she turned a page, a scrap of paper fluttered free, catching the light as it floated to the floor. She frowned, reaching down to pick it up. It was folded several times, and when she carefully opened it, her breath caught.

It was a note. Written in biro, the ink slightly faded but unmistakably in her dad's tidy, deliberate handwriting:

'Paramedic. Didn't act. Just watched. Not enough info. Something not right. Call Davies in morning.'

Her hand trembled slightly. The words echoed in her head like a dropped stone in still water. He'd seen it. Seen him.

She looked over at her mam, still dozing gently under the throw, unaware of the revelation now burning a hole in her daughter's palm.

Maddy lowered herself onto the floor beside the coffee table, legs folded under her, and stared at the note again. The date in the corner placed it shortly before her dad died. It wasn't much, but it was something. A whisper from the grave, telling her she wasn't alone in seeing what Daniel Cross truly was. Her dad had known. He might not have had the proof, but he'd felt the wrongness too.

"You saw it, didn't you?" she murmured, voice barely audible. Her eyes prickled, but she blinked the sting away. "You saw him."

* * *

Later in her room, she pinned the printout of Elena's photo next to Sophie's, drew a line, then another. One to Sarah Denton-Cross. One to her dad's note.

The map of Whitby was threaded now. A web of red lines, of women, men, and what-ifs. Each pin held a weight, each connection a thread of lives intertwined by a Paramedic's obsession. She stood there, the quiet of her room amplifying the heaviness in her chest.

Her arms folded across herself, holding it all in, but it didn't ease the tight knot behind her ribs. She didn't want it to. The ache kept her sharp.

"He's still hunting," she said quietly, the words more to herself than the empty room. "But now we're hunting him back."

It wasn't bravado. It wasn't a declaration. It was a promise Quiet yet unwavering.

Chapter Twenty-Three

The Duke of York was busier than usual for a weekday evening. The low hum of conversation filled the snug pub perched high above the harbour, its windows overlooking the dark sweep of the North Sea. Outside, the wind rattled against the glass, carrying with it the sharp tang of seaweed. Inside the old building the air was warm, heavy with the scent of ale and frying chips. Fishermen hunched at the bar with pints of bitter, voices low and rough with laughter. Locals crowded into corners, catching up on gossip, their words drowned by the scrape of chairs and the clink of glasses.

Maddy and Jack had taken a table near the window, half-shadowed by the glow of the wall sconce above them. The view was wasted on her. Her eyes barely left the condensation slipping down the side of her coke glass, fingers tapping an anxious rhythm against its base. Jack had insisted on a quiet drink, just a catch-up. But she'd known the moment he suggested it that he had something more in mind.

He watched her over the rim of his pint, his expression calm but with that familiar glint that said he wasn't letting her off easy. "You're a mile away again, Frosty. Care to tell me where your head's wandered off to this time?"

She sighed, leaning back against the worn leather seat. "It's always the same place these days. That paramedic. The victims. My dad. Like I'm on some obsession carousel."

Jack set his pint down carefully. "Then get off. Take a breath, Mads. You're no good to anyone if you run yourself into the ground."

"I don't have the luxury of breathers, Jack, you must remember that. Not while he's out there."

Jack leaned in, elbows resting on the table. His tone softened, but his words were firm. "You've been hunting him on his terms. You said it yourself, he's always watching. Always one step ahead. So why don't you stop trying to chase him and make him come to you?"

She frowned. "You think we haven't tried baiting him?"

"Not properly. You've been waiting for him to make a mistake. But you could give him something he can't resist." Jack's eyes didn't waver. "You said he's obsessed with these Sarah lookalikes. What if you put one right under his nose?"

Maddy's stomach tightened. "We can't use a civilian, Jack. I'm not feeding someone to a shark."

"I'm not suggesting you do. But you've got press connections, don't you? Subtle leaks. Controlled information. Let him think he's found a crack in the armour. You're clever enough to manage that without risking a civilian. Right now, you're showing him what *you* want him to see. What if you showed him what *he* wants to see instead?"

He let the words hang, and Maddy sat back, the idea settling like a weight on her chest.

"You're thinking media," she said.

Jack smiled. "You've got a journalist in your pocket, haven't you?"

Maddy's mind was already whirring, gears shifting. "Tom Denton."

"Exactly."

*　*　*

The café they picked was the Jet Black Jewel Café on Skinner Street, part of the boutique hotel of the same name. It wasn't the kind of place anyone would expect to find a police meeting. That was the point. The interior was all deep hues and warm lighting, with lanterns strung from dark beams overhead, the scent of fresh-ground coffee laced with something sweeter, cinnamon, maybe. A place for tourists, couples, or friends catching up, not detectives conspiring with journalists.

Tom was already there, hunched over a black coffee, his laptop open in front of him. He looked up as Maddy and Emily walked over, drawing his gaze.

"You've got that look, Mads. The one that means I'm about to regret this meeting," he said, pushing his glasses up his nose. "This is starting to feel like a full-time job." He still wore a plaster over his forehead, but much smaller than the bandage he had sported the last time Maddy had seen him. The other side of his face was now looking like he hadn't slept for a few nights, instead of been battered by a fist.

He watched them both slide into the booth.

"You'll live," Maddy replied with a small smile, pulling out a folder and laying it between them. "Look, we really need you to write another piece like before. Just a quiet one this time, no fanfare. It needs to be buried beneath the usual noise. Like a human-interest piece about a survivor who's been working with the police. Someone who perhaps had an accident similar to his wife, Sarah. It needs to be subtle enough not to spook him but tempting enough that he'll take the bait."

Tom leaned back, arms crossed. "So basically, you want me to write a story designed to provoke a serial killer? You do know that's not exactly standard journalism protocol, right?"

"You've danced this line before, Tom," Maddy shot back, giving him a desperate look. "I need you to dance it again. Just one more time. Without you, I'm not sure if we have any more avenues to tread."

Tom rubbed a hand over his face, exhaling heavily. She knew he was torn, but there was a part of him that would still probably do anything for her. "Fine," he breathed eventually. "I'm in. But we do this my way. Subtle, okay? No flashy headlines and no obvious tells. We need him to think he's spotted something that we've missed. You know, a weakness, not that we're waving bait in his face. That's how you get a man like him to move."

Maddy smiled thinly. "Deal."

* * *

By the afternoon, Maddy was back at the station, unable to sit still. She feared she might wear a groove into the floor as she paced in front of Emily's desk, her shoulders tight, her jaw set. Every few seconds she checked the time on the wall clock, as though that would hurry the process along. The final draft of the article was going to print, Tom's words sharpened and sanded just enough to slip past unnoticed by most—but not by the paramedic. That was the gamble. The plan was deliberately simple: Make him think information had leaked out the side door of the investigation. Give him just enough to convince himself he was cleverer than them. Let him believe he had the upper hand.

Emily tracked her with her eyes, one eyebrow raised, pen

tapping on the desk. "This feels thin, Mads. We're banking on him even noticing it. Or even caring enough to act."

"He will," Maddy said, her voice clipped but steady. She stopped long enough to lean across the desk. "If we're right, and he's been looking for Sarah in every woman he's watched, then this will feel like a thread dangling right in front of him. He won't be able to resist tugging."

Emily exhaled and pushed her chair back, folding her arms. "Alright. Fine. But what's our coverage plan? Because right now it feels like we're throwing a scrap into the water and hoping a shark swims by."

Maddy straightened, crossing her arms to stop herself from fidgeting. "No decoys. I'm the bait."

Emily blinked, then sat forward sharply. "That's not a plan, that's a suicide note."

"It's calculated risk," Maddy shot back, the words coming fast. "He won't come at me head-on. That's not his style. He'll circle first, test the ground, watch for weakness. But when he does, when he makes that move, we'll know exactly where he is."

The tension between them was still thick when Harper strode past. He caught the tail end of the exchange, enough to stop and fold his arms, his eyes narrowing. "Frost, you're walking a line so thin it might as well be the edge of a knife."

Maddy met his gaze without flinching. "I know, sir."

Harper rubbed at his temples as if she were the cause of his headache. "Fine. But this is your last gamble. I mean it. One more stunt with the press, and you're finished. Make this count, or it'll be on your head."

That evening, Maddy returned home to find her mam in the kitchen, brewing a pot of tea. The soft clink of china was a familiar comfort after the day's tension, and the faint smell of dinner still hung in the air. Her mam's hands moved with quiet purpose, pouring boiling water over the teabags, her expression softening when she saw her daughter.

"You look knackered," her mam said, pushing a cup towards her. "Like you've been carrying the whole world on your back again."

Maddy took it gratefully, sinking into a chair. The heat seeped into her palms as she cradled the mug. "We're trying something new. Something risky." Her voice came out low, worn, as if the words themselves carried weight.

Claire gave her a look that was half-concern, half-understanding, lips pressing into a thin line. "You've been living with risk since you took the badge, love. Just don't lose yourself in it. No job's worth that. Not even yours."

Maddy managed a tired smile, eyes stinging more than she cared to admit. "I'm trying, Mam. I really am."

Her mam reached across the table, covering her hand with a warm, steady grip. "Then that's all you can do."

They sat in silence for a while, the warmth of the tea easing some of the day's weight, and the tick of the kitchen clock filling the spaces between their breaths. For the first time that day, Maddy felt the sharp edges of her thoughts soften, if only for a moment.

* * *

The article went live later that night. No headlines. No bold claims. Just a quiet feature buried in the community news about a woman who survived a near-fatal crash and had been helping police with ongoing investigations.

Maddy didn't sleep. Neither did Emily. The next two days were spent in tense vigilance, monitoring calls and lines, waiting for any sign that Daniel had taken the bait. It had been busy, but that morning felt different, quieter in some ways, but still edged with an expectation that made Maddy's skin prickle.

The call came at 5:46am. Emily's voice was sharp but calm.

"He's been. Someone from the early morning harbour patrol spotted it and rang it in. A white rose with a small cross on it, left right on the memorial plaque for your dad outside the station entrance. Everyone who passes there knows it. He wanted it to be obvious, Mads. No note, no prints, just the rose."

Maddy stilled, the quiet of her bedroom pressing in as the weight of the words landed. Her gaze flicked to the window, the first pale light of morning soft against the curtains. For a long moment, she said nothing, the sound of her own breathing loud in her ears.

"No note?"

"None. Just the rose. No prints either. Forensics already checked."

That made it worse. Deliberate. Careful. A message meant for her and no one else.

Maddy exhaled slowly, her throat tight. "He's watching."

Emily's voice was grim. "Yeah. And he wants you to know it."

For years, Daniel had operated in the shadow, patient and methodical. But Maddy had done what no one else had managed: she'd seen the pattern, connected the deaths and refused to let it go. Her father had been close too, his old notebooks proved that. He'd circled Daniel's name, added question marks, sensed something wrong. Perhaps that's what had made Daniel nervous enough to escalate back then, too.

For someone who believed in fate's grand design, being exposed by detectives who wouldn't accept his philosophy must have felt like a personal affront. First her father, now her. She'd backed him into a corner, and cornered predators always lashed out. The rose wasn't sudden. It was inevitable.

Maddy straightened on the edge of the bed, pushing her hair back from her face as if to steel herself. "Then we make our move where he can see it too."

Chapter Twenty-Four

The station felt different that morning. Not quieter, exactly, but heavy, as if the air itself had thickened overnight. The phones still rang and the keyboards still clattered, but the rhythm was off, like a song played out of tune. It was the morning after the failed trap, and the fallout lingered like smoke after a house fire, acrid and clinging to everything. Even the smell of the overworked coffee machine seemed sharper, burnt. Conversations were hushed, officers moving about with the distracted focus of people unwilling to meet each other's eyes.

Maddy sat slumped at her desk, her gaze fixed on the evidence board pinned to the far wall. The photographs and notes blurred if she stared too long, her mind refusing to make connections. What held her instead was the clear evidence bag resting in the corner of her desk. Inside, the white rose lay perfectly preserved, its petals unmarked, fragile. It looked more suited to a wedding bouquet than a police station. But Maddy knew better. It wasn't just a flower; it was Daniel Cross' way of clawing himself into her thoughts. He had chosen her dad's memorial plaque, outside the station where every copper and every passer-by would see it. A deliberate strike, personal and cruel.

The scrape of leather soles on linoleum cut through her thoughts. Harper's stride was unmistakable, brisk and deliberate. He stopped by her desk, hands planted on his hips. His expression gave nothing away, but his jaw was set tight.

"You're too close, Frost." His voice was calm but clipped. "But I'd rather have you inside the tent than blowing holes in it from the outside."

Maddy dragged her gaze from the rose to meet his eyes. "I can handle it, sir."

Harper's stare lingered on her for a beat, the kind that made most officers squirm. Then he rubbed the back of his neck, sighing. "You need to rein it in. No more games with that journalist, no more lone-wolf heroics. You hear me? You're part of a team, and if you go rogue again, you won't just tank your career, you'll drag the rest of us down with you." He paused, eyes narrowing as he sighed. "But I know you. You won't stop. So whatever you do next, make sure it doesn't blow back on us. Understood?"

Maddy gave the smallest of nods. It was the closest thing to permission she was going to get.

The next morning, Maddy found Emily already leaning against her desk, a paper cup of coffee in hand. The smell hit before Maddy even sat down, bitter and burnt. Emily's wry smile did little to make up for the dark circles under her eyes.

"Brought you one," Emily said, sliding the second cup towards her. "Don't get too excited…it tastes like tar."

Maddy raised the lid, inhaled, and winced. "You weren't exaggerating."

"Punishment," Emily said lightly, though her expression turned serious. "For dragging me into your hair-brained schemes. He's watching. He's taunting. But he's slipping, Mads."

Maddy traced a finger round the rim of the cup, thoughtful. "Or maybe we're just dancing to his rhythm. He leads, we follow. Puppets on a string."

Emily leaned closer, her tone dropping. "Then we cut the strings. That business with the rose at your dad's plaque...it's too deliberate. It fits his pattern, right down to the timing. If we wait, he'll choose the next one for us."

They went back and forth, voices low but urgent. Emily pointing out the inconsistencies, Maddy arguing that Daniel Cross was setting the tempo. Their frustration built, both of them pacing, snapping at each other, then lapsing into silence before starting again. Eventually Emily stood at the whiteboard, scribbling names, dates, times, trying to impose order on chaos.

"It's all in here," Emily muttered, tapping the pen against her temple.

Maddy slumped into the chair, rubbing her eyes. "Or he's keeping us just far enough behind to stay ahead. That's the game."

For a long moment, they stared at the board together, the scrawled lines and red circles telling a story they couldn't yet prove.

* * *

Dr. Vishaal Patel arrived mid-morning, a file tucked firmly under one arm, glasses slipping precariously down his nose. He looked as though he'd had little sleep, shirt rumpled, but there was a spark of purpose in his eyes. He set the thick report on her desk with a deliberate thump, louder than necessary, making both women glance up.

"I've got something," he said, voice pitched low but urgent, eyes bright despite the smudges of fatigue beneath them. "There's a common thread in the chemical suppressants from the tox screens. They link back to an experimental trauma trial at York Hospital about ten years ago." He paused, drawing in a breath, letting the weight of the words settle into the room before he continued. "A trial Daniel Cross attended."

Maddy straightened at once, sharp with interest, her chair squeaking as she shifted forward. "You're sure? Absolutely sure?"

The coroner tapped the edge of the file with one blunt finger. "As sure as I can be without his medical records. The compounds match. Rare enough that they don't crop up anywhere else. These aren't run-of-the-mill sedatives; they were tailored for that study."

Maddy frowned. "But how does he get access to them after they're admitted? Hospital security, visitor logs..."

"He doesn't need to sneak in," Patel said. "He's a registered paramedic. He can walk into most NHS facilities in uniform and no one questions it. Checking on a patient he brought in is perfectly legitimate. And if he times it for shift changes or busy periods..." He let the implication hang.

"So he just walks in, uniform on, confident, and everyone assumes he belongs there," Emily said quietly.

"Exactly. Medical staff trust other medical staff. It's how hospitals function. And Daniel's been doing this long enough to know exactly when and how to blend in."

Emily was already fishing her phone from her pocket, her movements quick, almost jittery. "My dad's still got contacts from the ambulance service. Old-timers who'll remember who rotated where. I'll see if they can confirm Daniel was on shift during that period." Her thumbs hovered above the screen as though she was fighting the urge to text there and then.

Dr. Patel's tone cooled, the professional caution slipping

back into place. "Careful. Hearsay might steer us, but formal warrants will be needed if you want anything that'll stand. Tread lightly until Harper signs off." He adjusted his glasses, glancing between the two of them with the air of a man who had dropped a stone into water and was waiting for the ripples.

Maddy leaned back, pulse quickening despite the exhaustion dragging at her bones. For the first time in days, she felt a flicker of progress spark in her chest. It wasn't just suspicion any more, it was something tangible, a thread she could grip and tug. A link tying Daniel to his victims, and maybe, if they worked fast enough, to his next move.

* * *

That afternoon, Jack turned up at the station reception with a takeaway bag dangling from one hand. He looked out of place amongst the uniforms milling about near the desk, rougher and more weathered than the pressed shirts and polished boots around him, but he waited without fuss until Maddy came down the stairs to meet him. A few of the younger constables glanced his way with curiosity, nudging each other, and he pretended not to notice. As soon as she reached him, he lifted the bag towards her with a faint grin.

"You look like you've been chewing nails," he said, folding his arms across his chest in mock disapproval. "Thought you could use something edible before you grind your teeth to dust."

Maddy arched a brow, tugging the bag open. A bacon butty, still warm, the smell filling the foyer and instantly cutting through the stale tang of coffee and disinfectant. For the first time that day, she managed a real smile. "Feels like it, aye. You might've just saved my life."

They wandered out the front and perched on a nearby bench, the late afternoon light casting long shadows across the pavement. Jack watched her with quiet patience as she took the first bite, crumbs catching at her lips. "However much you try to act like it, you've still got people around you, you know," he reassured her.

She swallowed slowly, the lump in her throat making it harder than it should have been. "I know," she said softly, though the words carried more weight than she meant them to.

Jack let the silence stretch, the sounds of gulls overhead and the hum of traffic filling the space. He didn't press, he never did. Just sat steady as stone beside her, offering that grounding presence she hadn't even realised she needed. It wasn't a grand gesture, but it was enough to ease something tight inside her chest.

* * *

By evening, the office had thinned, leaving a low murmur of phones and the occasional crackle from the radio bank. The strip lights hummed. The whiteboard smelled faintly of solvent from earlier, where someone had scrubbed a corner clean and left a milky tide mark. Maddy and Emily had commandeered a cluster of desks by the window, papers fanned out like a hand of bad cards, laptop cables snaking over staplers and empty mugs.

"Right," Emily said, uncapping a pen with her teeth. "One more pass. No shortcuts."

Maddy pulled a fresh sheet towards her and began drawing a timeline in long, steady strokes. "Victims in black. Daniel Cross' rota in blue. Dr. Patel's trial data in red." She was speaking to keep herself moving as much as to brief Emily. Fatigue made everything feel heavy. The pen weighed more than it should, and the paper dragged under her palm.

Emily tapped at her keyboard, pulling up a rota ledger they had no business having. "Here. York Hospital trauma trial, ten years ago. Daniel Cross signed in on these teaching days." She slid a printout across. "Not proof, though it is something."

"Something is fine," Maddy said. "We can turn something into evidence."

They worked in near silence for a few minutes. The squeak of the drywipe pen, the scratch of biro, the distant clunk of the heating pipes starting up. Outside the glass, the corridor lights clicked off in sections where no one had moved for a while, plunging patches of the station into grey.

Emily broke the quiet. "Okay, let's assume we're right about his progression. He attends the trial, learns the pharmacology, and then, for years, he sits with survivors. He talks to them. Watches and doesn't touch. Not yet." She circled two dates. "Then, four years ago, he started choosing. Quietly. One every few months."

Maddy rubbed a thumb along the edge of a printout, feeling the rough cut against her skin. "Choosing is the word." She pointed to names, each one a weight. "Sophie Chambers. Peter Longstaff. Tessa North. All survived something first."

"And all in catchment areas where he either worked or volunteered." Emily's tone had flattened into the careful cadence she used when the shape of a thing emerged. "Look at this overlap here." She drew a neat box around a fortnight in early spring. "Each year, there's a gap in his rota. He takes leave."

Maddy frowned. "Annual leave isn't illegal."

"No," Emily said, "but look at when he takes it." She reached for a file, flicked to a photocopied obituary, then another. Her pen tapped a date printed in small type along the bottom. "The anniversary of Sarah Denton-Cross' death sits inside that window."

The name landed in the space between them. Maddy felt

the familiar pull in her chest, like she'd stepped too close to a cliff edge.

"Coincidence?" Emily asked, though her voice suggested she didn't believe it.

Maddy studied the timeline. The red, the blue, the black. "It seems like he's ritualising," she said quietly. "Like he tells himself a story each year and then he writes another ending for someone else."

Emily leaned back, folding her arms. "We take this to Harper first thing. Get him to green-light warrants for supply logs and rota confirmations. If we catch him drawing the same pattern again, we put cars where he'll be."

"We need more than cars," Maddy said. She could feel the old itch under her skin, the same urge that had once taken her to the south, determined to make a name for herself. She wanted to run ahead and drag the truth into daylight with her bare hands. She forced her voice to stay even. "We need eyes on the ambulance dispatch channel, a liaison in control willing to flag near misses that match his type. We don't wait for a body."

Emily gave her a sideways look. "You're asking to stand in front of a moving train."

"I am asking to be on the platform when it pulls in," Maddy replied. "Big difference."

They fell into another spell of work. Emily built a spreadsheet with columns that turned chaotic notes into something crisp. Maddy lifted photos from the board and laid them flat, lining edges, removing duplicates, trimming away noise until only the necessary remained. She jotted questions in the margin of her pad. Who did he visit off rota. Which wards ignored visitor protocols. Who remembers a paramedic who did not belong.

A printer coughed somewhere behind them, spitting out a

constable's shift pattern. The vending machine in the corridor rattled and gave up on swallowing a pound coin. The station had its own nighttime music and, for once, it steadied her.

Emily's voice softened. "Do you ever feel like we are chasing a shadow on a wall?"

"All the time," Maddy said. "But shadows need light. Find the light and the shape shows itself."

Emily nodded at the board. "Light, then." She drew a thin circle around a date three days away. She wrote one word beside it in small, neat letters. 'Anniversary'.

The word sat there, sharp as glass.

Maddy capped her pen, then uncapped it again. She stepped to the board and made the same circle with a red marker, slower, pressing just hard enough for the ink to bite into the gloss. The room seemed to hold its breath.

"What do we tell Harper in the morning?" Emily asked.

"The truth," Maddy said. "That we have a window and a pattern and a man who does not deviate once he's taught himself the story." She replaced the cap, set the pen down so the nib would not dry out, and gathered the loose pages into a tidy stack as if order on the desk might make order in her head.

Emily closed the laptop with a careful click. "Then we plan for that date."

Maddy glanced to the corner of her desk where the bagged rose lay. She turned the evidence bag face down. "Aye," she said. "We plan."

The motion sensor cut the lights to a lower setting, washing the office in soft grey. For a moment neither of them spoke. Somewhere along the corridor a kettle began to boil, thin steam squealing through a lid that did not fit. She checked the time on her phone and slid it back into her pocket without looking at the notifications that stacked the screen.

"See you first thing," Emily said.

"First thing," Maddy replied, and the words felt solid enough to stand on.

Chapter Twenty-Five

The next morning, the station carried a different weight. Not the weary hush of defeat, but the tense, breathless energy of a case about to tip. The phones rang continuously, footsteps hurried through the corridors, and the whiteboard in CID had been stripped back and overlaid with fresh notes. Red circles, blue lines, Patel's toxicology results, all of it layered with Emily's rota printouts.

The air itself seemed taut, stretched thin with the sense that something was about to break. This was the day they took it upstairs to Harper and asked him to put his name on the line.

Maddy sat at her desk, pen tapping restlessly against her notebook. She'd barely slept, her mind replaying Daniel Cross' smirk, the damned white rose and her mam's worried face. Every detail seemed sharper in the daylight, as though her exhaustion had peeled away whatever defences she normally held. When Emily appeared with two mugs of coffee, steam curling around her, she slid one over with a sympathetic grin.

"You look like death warmed up."

"Always a charmer," Maddy muttered, taking a gulp that scalded her tongue but forced her awake. "Ready?"

Emily didn't answer straight-away. She simply raised her eyebrows, the look saying everything: ready or not, it was time. Harper's door creaked open a moment later, and he crooked a finger at them like a schoolmaster calling in his naughty pupils. The sound of the latch clicking behind them might as well have been a lock on a cell door.

Harper's office smelled faintly of stale tobacco and old paper, like the inside of a university library that no one had dusted in years. The blinds cut the light into sharp stripes, leaving half his desk in shadow. The superior sat behind it, sleeves rolled up, glasses perched low, pen in hand but unmoving. A file lay open before him, but his gaze was fixed on them and nothing else.

"Well? Let's hear it."

Emily stepped forward, marker in hand. She pulled the whiteboard closer, the wheels squealing across the lino, and pointed to the victim dates and rota absences.

"Daniel Cross isn't striking at random," she started. "He's aligning his victims with anniversaries, his shifts, and gaps in his rota. Dr. Patel's tox results confirm suppressant compounds...rare ones...that trace back to a York Hospital trauma trial. And lo and behold? Our paramedic was on rotation at York Hospital at that exact time."

Harper's face gave nothing away. He leaned back, chair creaking, jaw tight. Maddy could feel her own pulse in her throat, her voice steadier than she felt as she added, "This isn't a theory any more, sir. It's a pattern with forensic backing. We're asking for warrants. His paramedic supply logs, rota confirmations, dispatch records. If we get access, we'll have him."

The silence stretched long enough that Maddy's palms began to sweat, her pen digging a faint mark into the side of her notebook. Emily didn't shift, didn't blink, just stared Harper down like she'd burn through him if she had to.

A moment passed. Then another before DI Harper exhaled, slow and heavy.

"You realise what you're asking? You want me to put my name behind accusing a popular, locally loved paramedic of being a serial killer. If we put this in front of a judge and it falls apart, it's not just your jobs...it's mine."

Emily met his stare, chin lifted. "And if we don't, people keep dying. That's the choice."

Harper rubbed his temple, then snapped the file shut with a crack that echoed. He pushed his chair back, stood, and jabbed his pen towards the door. "Fine. You'll get your warrants but keep it quiet. The last thing we need is your paramedic sniffing the wind before we're ready."

Relief cut through Maddy, sharp and dizzying. Harper's sign-off wasn't warm, but it was enough. The net was finally tightening, and for once, it felt like they were finally closing in.

The paperwork fell to Emily. She had the knack for it, the precise language, the legal phrasing, and the dogged patience for bureaucracy. Maddy trailed her through the process, watching her tap out the details on the system: trial data, rota records, supply access.

DI Harper's name went onto the forms, his grudging signature looping at the bottom with a promise to pull as many strings as he could to get a response asap. Then it was out of their hands, sent into the slow-turning cogs of the legal machine.

Waiting was its own kind of torture. The station had taken on the strange hush that only comes when everyone's trying to pretend they're not tense. Every tick of the clock drilled into Maddy's skull, sharp and relentless. The radiator hissed and clanked. A kettle clicked off somewhere down the corridor. A low mumble of voices carried from CID, but the incident room itself felt like a vacuum.

Maddy paced, back and forth, shoes scuffing the floor tiles.

She'd lost count of how many steps it had been. Ten across, ten back. Her hands itched for something to do, but all the evidence had been logged and labelled, the rota charts aligned, the paperwork filed. Now they just had to wait.

Emily sat nearby, stiff-backed in a chair that looked more punishing by the minute, arms folded tightly across her chest. She wasn't speaking, wasn't fidgeting, but her eyes kept darting to her watch in the most unsubtle way possible. Every few minutes, she shifted and resettled her shoulders.

Dr. Patel joined them eventually, his footsteps soft but precise as he entered with a quiet air of purpose, his files balanced under one arm and the faint aroma of mint tea clinging to him. His glasses were already halfway down his nose before he'd sat down, and he didn't bother pushing them back up. Just being in the room with him calmed something in Maddy's chest. He never rushed, never panicked. There was a steadiness in him that balanced out all the chaos.

This time, however, his calmness was short-lived as the phone rang before he had a chance to sit down. Emily lunged for it and held it to her ear for a moment. Her expression shifted as she listened, tension melting into something else...triumph, maybe.

When she hung up, she didn't say anything at first. Just turned, holding up the page that had printed through behind her like it was a trophy.

"Warrants are granted," she said, her voice somewhere between a breath and a laugh. "We've bloody got them." She dropped into the chair beside Maddy with a whoosh of air, waved the official page like a certificate and sighed, "I should frame this. Stick it up in the loo. Remind myself bureaucracy occasionally works. And a special thanks to Harper getting this sign off fast-tracked direct with the Crown Court!"

Maddy couldn't help it. A grin tugged at the edge of her mouth.

Dr. Patel raised a dry eyebrow, then stepped forward and dropped his file onto the table with a satisfying thud. Finally able to show what he came for. "The suppressant compounds found in the toxicology screens? They match exactly to a single batch used in the York trauma trial. Limited batch, tightly controlled. Only a handful of staff had access."

Maddy's breath caught, and Emily leaned in as he turned the file around, the top page showing dates, patient codes, and Daniel Cross' name in the margins.

"This guy was on rota that week. No question about it," Dr. Patel said, tapping the paper. "That's your forensic link."

The noise in the station carried on beyond their door, but inside that room, it felt as though something had shifted, like the entire case had just realigned into something solid.

Emily nodded slowly, gripping the warrant tighter. "Now we've got him. Properly."

Maddy didn't answer. She didn't need to. Her stomach was already tightening. Because if they could feel the trap closing, then surely Daniel Cross could too.

* * *

Emily leaned across the desk, her finger tracing the overlapping lines on the rota overlay until her fingertip smudged the ink.

"Look at this. Every one of his strikes ties back into dates linked with his wife. But here—" She circled one particular date with the marker, the squeak loud in the silence, the smell of solvent sharp in the air. "The anniversary of Sarah Cross' death. It's in three days. If he's going to act, it'll be then."

A shiver worked its way down Maddy's spine, a cold ripple that had nothing to do with the draught sneaking under the door. Her arms prickled with goose-flesh, and she wrapped them tight across her chest. She hadn't needed Emily to say it; the pattern was already there in her gut, unavoidable, a knot she couldn't untie. She glanced at the clock, at the sunlight falling in angled shards through the grimy window, as everything suddenly too bright, too sharp.

Harper leaned forward, elbows on the desk, his expression harder than before, the weight of command pressing through his words. His pen tapped once, twice, against the wood before he stilled it.

"Fine," he said at last. "We'll authorise surveillance. No grand gestures, no media leaks. Plainclothes only. We need to keep eyes on potential targets that match his usual profile. If he so much as breathes in their direction, I want to know."

Maddy and Emily exchanged a glance, a flicker of shared tension and silent understanding. The look carried everything: fear, determination, and the thin thread of trust between them.

Maddy swallowed, her throat dry as the sounds of the station seeped in faintly through the closed door. It wasn't enough, not to her, but it was the best they'd get. The countdown had started and each second brought her closer to taking him down.

* * *

That evening, Maddy trudged home, shoulders heavy. The house smelled of stew, enough to comfort her senses and as much as she needed to move out and find her own place, she would never tire of seeing her mam busying about in the kitchen.

The window was open a crack, letting in the sound of gulls and the faint tang of salt air. Claire looked up as Maddy came in, eyes narrowing immediately.

"Everything okay?" she asked, wiping her hands on a tea towel. "I sent you a message earlier but didn't hear anything back."

Maddy dropped her bag by the door with a dull thud. "Sorry, Mam, I got a bit caught up at work and then we had to wait on warrants and stuff, but I'm just shattered now."

Claire shook her head, setting a plate down on the table with more force than necessary. "Sit. Eat. You can't fight anything on an empty stomach. Don't argue." She added the last part knowing the protest she would usually receive.

This time however, Maddy did as she was told, though she only managed a few mouthfuls before pushing the plate away. Her mam's eyes followed her the whole time, soft but insistent.

In that silence, with the telly in the background and the old clock ticking on the mantel, Maddy felt the weight of everything pressing down harder than it did at the station. She was still someone's daughter, still tethered to a kitchen table, and somehow that made the burden sharper.

Her phone buzzed later, just as she was rinsing her plate and letting the hot water run over her fingers until they reddened. A text from Jack lit up the screen, the words stark against the glow in the dim kitchen:

Heard things were heating up. Need a pint? Or at least a chat?

She hesitated, thumb hovering above the glass, heart thudding at the thought of his voice. For a moment she thought about ignoring it, about pretending she hadn't seen the message, but the silence in the house pressed too hard and she was starting to find that she craved his wisdom and carefree advice. It wasn't too late to meet him, but she couldn't stomach the idea of heading out again. She called him instead.

He answered on the second ring, his voice rough with the sea air and the background noise of wind. She could picture him there on the harbour wall, phone crooked against his shoulder, one hand shoved into his jacket pocket.

"Frosty." He answered.

"Don't call me that." She could hear the smile in his silence, the pause saying more than words. She leaned against the counter, staring at the dripping tap. "What can I do you for?"

"Just checking you're still upright." He cleared his throat. "Word gets around, even down on the pier. Don't try and take this bloke on alone. He's not the sea...you can't just weather him out." His voice carried that easy authority of someone who had spent years fighting the tide, someone who knew how unforgiving it could be.

Despite herself, Maddy let out a small laugh, the sound cracking something tight in her chest. "You always did have a way with metaphors."

Jack chuckled low, then grew quieter, steadier, as if choosing his words carefully. "Look after yourself, eh? Your mam would never forgive me if I didn't say that."

Her throat tightened. She wanted to tell him she was fine, but the words stuck, unconvincing even to herself. Instead she traced the edge of the plate in the rack, condensation gathering beneath her palm. She didn't promise him anything. Couldn't. But he was a welcome, momentary distraction.

When the call ended, the quiet in the kitchen settled heavier than before. The shadows stretched long across the ceiling as if even they were waiting, and the faint echo of gulls outside the window made the silence feel even deeper, the absence of his voice almost louder than the brief conversation had been.

* * *

By evening the next day, the briefing room was full, charged with the nervous electricity of officers trying not to show excitement. Harper stood at the front, flanked by the whiteboard and rota overlays, which now bore an increasing sprawl of red marker lines and sticky notes. The evidence board, dense with photographs and timelines, gave the impression of a case on the verge of breaking open, or exploding.

Officers leaned against the walls, some cross-armed, others flipping through notepads. One constable balanced a paper cup of coffee on his knee, eyes glued to the rota as though it held secrets he hadn't yet cracked.

The air was thick with anticipation and fatigue. The scrape of chairs being adjusted, the quiet rustle of notes changing hands, and the creak of boots shifting weight across the lino floor, all melded into a tense background noise.

Harper cleared his throat, silencing the room with a glance.

"Surveillance rotations are set," he began, his voice cutting through the atmosphere with clipped authority. "Plainclothes only. I don't want anything that even smells like uniform on this. Vishaal will liaise with the medical response teams in case anything crops up at hospital level. Frost, Ward, you're on the sharp end. Closest to potential targets. If Daniel Cross moves, you'll be the first to feel it."

A ripple of tension passed through the crowd, shoulders tensing, heads dipping as instructions were absorbed and mentally filed.

Maddy nodded automatically, though her stomach twisted in protest, the muscles tight as piano wire. Across from her, Emily gave a tight smile. Her jaw clenched visibly, shoulders drawn back with rigid determination.

They were both too deep now to retreat. The net they'd helped weave was closing, and they were standing in the dead centre of it.

On the desk in front of Maddy, sealed in its clear plastic evidence bag, lay the white rose. It seemed out of place here, something delicate and ghostly among all the hard edges and acrid smells of anticipation, sweat, and stress. She couldn't stop staring at it. The petals were beginning to wilt slightly, browning at the edges. Her jaw locked tight, her fists clenched on her thighs hard enough to leave crescent marks from her nails. Her vision swam for a moment, blurring the pale edges of the rose into a white smear.

She forced herself to breathe through it. Slow, steady.

This time, she wouldn't let Daniel dictate the terms. Wouldn't let him steer the narrative. They were no longer chasing shadows or making guesses in the dark. They were ready. Almost.

Emily leaned slightly towards her, mumbling under her breath, "Three days. That's all we've got."

Maddy nodded, eyes never leaving the rose. "Then we'd better make them count."

Chapter Twenty-Six

The briefing room at Whitby Police Station smelled of stale coffee and damp coats, the sort of odour that clung to walls after too many winters. The blinds were still drawn against the early dawn light, the fluorescent strip buzzing overhead. Maddy sat at the back of the table, her notebook open but mostly blank, pen balanced between her fingers. Her head felt heavy, weighed down by too many nights of broken or no sleep at all. She rubbed at her eyes, forcing herself to focus.

Emily stood at the front with a map spread across the whiteboard. Red pins marked junctions and side streets, lines of black marker linking them together. She was brisk, efficient, her dark hair tied back, her voice clear as she explained the set-up. "We've got two unmarked cars here and here. Static cameras covering St Hilda's Terrace and Skinner Street. Plainclothes at the bus station. We rotate every three hours, no gaps."

Harper leaned against the wall, arms folded. He looked older than usual, the lines round his mouth deepening each time Emily spoke. When she finished, he cleared his throat.

"Listen carefully. Daniel Cross is clever. He won't show his face unless he thinks he's invisible. That means if he so much as smells us, we've wasted our chance. So make yourselves ghosts. No unnecessary chatter, no sudden moves." His eyes flicked to Maddy. "And no improvising."

She held his gaze, biting back the retort that rose. He wasn't wrong. But his warning stung all the same.

Her phone buzzed against the table. She glanced at the screen: a text from Jack. Good luck today. Watch your back. She swallowed and slid the phone face down. A folded note was tucked into her bag, written in her mam's neat handwriting: Catch him. But come home. Lunch in the fridge. The thought of leftovers waiting at home gave her the smallest pang in her chest, the reminder of a life that didn't revolve around A killer paramedic.

Emily sat down beside her, tapping her pen against her knee. "He's slippery, but today we're slicker."

"Let's hope so," Maddy muttered, forcing a thin smile.

By the time they took their positions, the drizzle had settled in, fine mist sticking to the windscreen of the unmarked Ford. Maddy sat in the passenger seat, notebook on her lap, radio clipped to her jacket. Emily was at the wheel, drumming her fingers against the steering wheel before catching herself and stopping.

The hospital car park stretched opposite them, puddles reflecting the dull light. People came and went with umbrellas, the occasional paramedic pushing a trolley through the rain. Every so often, one of the cameras on lampposts caught movement, relayed back to the surveillance team at the station.

The hours dragged. Maddy's thighs ached from sitting so still, her calves cramped against the floor of the car. The heater fogged the glass until Emily cracked the window an inch, letting in cold damp air that smelt faintly of sea salt. Maddy sipped at a paper cup of coffee gone lukewarm, forcing down another mouthful despite the bitter taste.

She kept replaying old memories. Her dad, sitting in his armchair years ago, telling her about stakeouts. *The hardest part isn't spotting the target, Mads. It's keeping your mind sharp when nothing happens.* He used to come home bone-tired, his voice hoarse, but proud when they'd made an arrest. She pressed her fingers against her temple, willing herself to focus.

Emily began to hum softly, something tuneless, almost absent-minded. It wormed its way under Maddy's skin until she snapped. "For God's sake, Em. Can you not?"

Emily startled, cheeks colouring. "Sorry. Nervous habit."

Maddy sighed, closing her eyes. "Forget it. Just...quiet, yeah?"

The rain thickened, pattering harder against the roof. A man in a grey hood crossed the street, and Maddy's chest tightened. She leaned forward, eyes narrowing. He pulled back his hood, revealing a head of thinning hair and a carrier bag full of groceries. Not him. Another woman trudged by with a pram. Not him either.

The clock on the dashboard ticked past two in the afternoon. Hours spent staring, logging shadows, scribbling down nothing of use. Her stomach growled; she ignored it. The drizzle blurred her vision, and she rubbed at the condensation on her side of the windscreen with the back of her sleeve.

It was nearly four when the radio crackled. "Target sighted. East corner, by the bus stop. Blue hoodie. Confirm?"

Maddy's head snapped up, eyes locking on the windscreen. Her pulse kicked hard, her fingers tightening on the edge of her seat. Emily leaned forward, narrowing her eyes at the grainy figure. He was moving at a steady pace, shoulders set, not wandering, and not rushing. Every line of his body suggested purpose.

Maddy grabbed the binoculars and steadied her hands. She forced herself to focus despite the tremor in her grip. Through the lenses, she caught the profile. Close-cropped greying hair, the lean angles of a face weathered by years on the job, early fifties but moving with the controlled precision of someone who knew exactly what he was doing. The outline of his jaw, the way his head tilted slightly forward in that calm, assessing manner she'd seen in the interview room. It was him. She felt the certainty settle heavily in her stomach, a thud of recognition. "It's him," she whispered. "Christ. It's him."

The radio crackled again with an urgent order. "Do not engage. Repeat. Do not engage."

Daniel reached the corner by the bus stop and paused. He adjusted his hood slightly and turned his head towards the line of parked cars, scanning without hurry. His movements were deliberate, his gaze sweeping over windscreens, taking in the street. His eyes passed over them and, for a brief moment, fixed on the windscreen of their vehicle. Maddy's breath caught and stayed locked in her chest. His posture didn't falter. He shifted his head a fraction, gave the faintest tilt as though acknowledging what he'd seen, then moved on, walking out of view with measured steps, his stride even and confident.

"Jesus," Emily breathed, voice tight. "He saw us."

"Hold position," Harper barked through the radio. "We're too exposed. No one moves." His words were clipped, controlled, but the edge of frustration was audible.

Maddy's hand clenched the door handle. Her body leaned forward, every muscle poised to get out and follow. "Sir, we can approach. Get a visual confirmation, at least."

A pause crackled through the radio. Then Harper's voice, tight with reluctance. "Frost, Ward, visual only. Do not spook him. Understood?"

"Understood." Maddy was already moving, easing the door

open quietly. Emily slipped out the passenger side, both of them keeping low, using parked cars for cover.

They moved carefully at first, crossing the street at an angle that kept them partially obscured. Daniel was still at the bus stop, hands in his pockets, appearing to check the timetable. Maddy's pulse hammered in her throat. Just a bit closer. Just enough to confirm it was him beyond any doubt.

Then he lifted his head. His gaze swept the street with practiced casualness and locked onto them for the briefest moment. Not surprise. Not fear. Just calm recognition, almost like he'd been waiting for this. Then he smiled, a small, deliberate curve of his mouth, and turned away.

"He's seen us," Emily breathed.

Daniel stepped backwards into the crowd gathering at the bus stop, moving with unhurried precision.

"We need to stop him before he bolts," Maddy said, picking up her pace. "Daniel Cross, we'd like a word."

But he was already moving, weaving through the passengers boarding the bus. Maddy broke into a run but he'd disappeared down a side alley between shops. She sprinted after him, rain slicking the pavement beneath her boots, Emily right behind her. When they rounded the corner, the alley opened onto three different directions: a car park, a residential street, and a narrow cut-through to the main road.

He was gone.

Maddy spun, scanning frantically. Nothing. Just wet concrete and the distant hum of traffic. Her radio crackled.

"Frost, report." Harper's voice was clipped.

Maddy pressed the button, trying to catch her breath. "He ran, sir. Lost him at the alley behind Church Street. Multiple exit routes."

"Get back here. Now."

Slowly, Maddy walked back to the car, frustration and rage

building with every step. Emily fell in beside her, saying nothing.

When they climbed back into the vehicle, Maddy slammed the door harder than necessary. "He's playing with us. He bloody knows." Her voice cracked with anger, the pressure of wasted hours and her own failed chase boiling over.

Emily reached across, hand brushing Maddy's arm. "We flushed him out. That means we're close."

"He's not afraid of us, Em. He's laughing at us." Maddy pressed her forehead against the glass, her breath misting the window. The mark of her helplessness still hanging in the air. A bus pulled up and passengers stepped off, but he was gone. Her breath misted the window again, leaving a cloudy patch that blurred the view, the mark of her helplessness still hanging in the air.

* * *

The station felt like a cave when they returned, lights glaring off the polished floor. Everyone looked hollow-eyed, carrying the weight of what they hadn't caught. In the incident room, DI Harper stood with arms folded while the footage replayed on loop. Daniel Cross' profile flickered briefly, grainy in the drizzle, before he turned away.

"It's him," Emily confirmed, voice firm. "He knew exactly where to look. Straight at us."

Harper stared at the frozen image, his jaw working. "We've got the York trial link, we've got Patel's toxicology." He exhaled sharply. "But visual confirmation of him walking down a street isn't enough for a warrant. We need him making a move. One mistake. That's all."

The others filed out one by one, muttering about schedules and reports, but Maddy stayed behind, her chair drawn close to the screen. She replayed the moment again and again, his eyes lifting toward the car. It wasn't a trick of the camera. He'd seen them. And he hadn't cared.

Her phone buzzed on the desk. Jack's name lit the screen. She let it ring, thumb hovering but never answering. Instead, she typed a quick message. Still breathing. Just. She hit send before she could change her mind.

Another message pinged. This one from her mam.

Come eat. You can fight fate better with left over stew in you.

Maddy stared at the phone, her throat tight. She shut her notebook, stuffed it into her bag, and took one last look at the frozen image on the screen. Daniel Cross, turning his back. Not a smile, not exactly. But something in the way he carried himself, as though he knew exactly how close he'd been and how powerless they were to stop him. That thought alone made her stomach knot.

Chapter Twenty-Seven

The station was barely awake when Emily burst through the doors, her hair damp from the early morning drizzle. The clock on the wall read just past six. Most of the team were still clutching their first mugs of tea, shoulders slouched, jackets still damp from the walk in. Emily's face had drained of colour, her expression set in a way that stripped the sleep from the room instantly. She carried her tablet close to her chest, breaths coming short and uneven as though she'd sprinted the whole way from her car.

"Maddy," she called across the incident room, her voice sharper than usual, louder than it needed to be. Everyone looked up. "Got him."

Maddy was on her feet before Emily had crossed the floor. The edge in her colleagues tone didn't leave any room for hesitation. "What happened?"

"A call came in from Goathland," Emily said quickly, her eyes flicking around at the others before fixing back on Maddy. "Semi-rural, head trauma, young woman in her twenties. Dark hair, pale skin." Her words tumbled out. "Paramedic on scene was Daniel Cross."

The noise in the room stilled to nothing. Even Harper, halfway through a mouthful of tea, lowered his cup slowly, his eyes narrowing. "How do you know for certain?"

Emily raised the tablet and spun it so they could see. CCTV stills filled the screen. Daniel stood outside a treatment room at Whitby Hospital, his hand pressed to the frosted glass. Emily's voice dropped slightly.

"The hospital confirmed he brought her in. But there's no record of that ambulance ever being dispatched," she explained. "It's not on the system. He bypassed the log and it looks like he's gone off their books."

Maddy's stomach clenched. She and Emily held each other's gaze. No words needed. This was the moment.

Harper set his mug down with a loud clunk. "He's broken cover. That's it. We end this today." His voice carried finality. No more hesitation.

The room snapped to life in an instant. Phones rang, chairs scraped back across the floor, and radios burst into a tangle of voices as officers began barking updates and relaying instructions. One officer started punching numbers into the switchboard, another scribbled details onto the incident board. The air thickened with movement and urgency.

Maddy shoved her chair back and grabbed her warrant card, sliding it into her jacket pocket. She could feel the tremor in her chest, the anticipation that this was the moment everything had built towards. She reached for the authorisation folder from Harper's desk, tucking it under her arm, its weight far heavier than paper ought to be. She checked her belt, clipped her radio into place, and patted down her pockets with a sharp efficiency to make sure she had what she needed.

Harper was barking orders at a sergeant by the door. "Get traffic units ready. No slip-ups. This is his only mistake and it'll be his last!" Officers moved around them in a blur, some pulling on high-vis jackets, others fitting earpieces. The hum of activity filled the room with a pressure that vibrated against Maddy's skin.

Emily was already at the door, holding it open with one hand, her face set with grim determination. "Come on, Mads, we're not going to lose him."

Maddy gave a short nod. Her boots struck the floor in heavy steps that echoed down the corridor. Behind them, the room still buzzed with action, but for Maddy everything narrowed to the single task ahead: catching Daniel Cross before he vanished again.

* * *

The Ford's tyres spat grit as Emily pushed it hard along the back lanes leading out of town. The narrow roads wound between hedgerows dripping with rain, the moorland beyond spreading wide and grey. Maddy kept the radio pressed to her mouth, her voice firm.

"All units, Cross was confirmed at Whitby Hospital within the last hour and was last seen outside the patient's room. Any sightings to be reported directly to me. Repeat, directly to me."

Emily's knuckles whitened around the wheel. "We can't let him vanish again. Not like yesterday."

Maddy kept her eyes on the road ahead. "We won't. Not this time. We stay with him, whatever it takes."

When they pulled into the hospital car park, the drizzle had turned to a steady rain. A nurse was waiting at the entrance, ushering them through with hurried steps. She looked nervous, glancing over her shoulder as though Daniel might be lurking inside. She led them straight to the security office, where grainy footage was already playing on a monitor. He was there, clear enough to recognise as he stood outside the treatment room, palm flat on the glass, trying to reach up and stare in though the open window.

"He didn't speak to anyone," the nurse said quickly. "He didn't ask any questions, just stood there for a few minutes then left."

Emily leaned closer to the screen, her jaw tight. "Maybe he's reliving it? Standing on the outside, watching her live or die just like Sarah."

Another staff member hurried in, voice low and urgent. "Sorry to interrupt," she breathed. "A porter saw him leaving through the east entrance about twenty minutes ago. Heading towards the clifftop path, down by the old lifeboat station."

Maddy grabbed the radio. "Harper, we've got a confirmed sighting. East exit, heading to the clifftop path near the lifeboat station."

"Understood," Harper's voice crackled back. "Backup en route. But you and Ward are closest. Keep your eyes on him. Don't lose him!"

Emily swung them back into the car, tyres screeching as they tore away from the hospital. Maddy braced herself with one hand on the dash. The streets of Whitby blurred past, shopfronts shuttered, pavements slick with rain. Maddy felt every corner like the tick of a clock.

* * *

The sea below the cliffs churned black and white, waves slamming against the rocks with force that shook the air. The wind carried spray upwards, stinging against skin and clothing. The path along the edge was slick, narrow, and treacherous. It was the kind of ground where one wrong step could send someone straight over.

Maddy spotted him first. Daniel Cross stood close to the

railing, his shoulders squared, rain dripping from his coat in steady rivulets. His hood was down, close-cropped greying hair darkened by the rain and plastered flat against his skull. The weathered lines of his face were sharper in the grey light, rain streaming down his cheeks and jaw, but his expression was utterly calm. Not defiant. Not afraid. Just waiting. His pale eyes tracked her approach with the same measured assessment she'd seen in the interview room, as though he were cataloguing every detail, every choice she'd made to bring her here. He didn't move when her footsteps crunched the gravel, though his head turned slightly, a faint tilt of acknowledgment.

"You came alone," he called over the rain. There was no surprise in his tone, only recognition. Almost satisfaction.

"You wanted me to," Maddy answered. Her steps were measured, deliberate, her shoulders squared. She stopped a safe distance away, her boots firm on the wet path. Her eyes stayed locked on his hands, watching for any twitch or sudden movement. The roar of the sea filled the silence between them. That mixed with the sound of the rain.

Daniel smiled faintly, but it didn't reach his eyes. "You've chased me for weeks. All that work, and here we are. Just us." He shifted slightly, as though testing the ground beneath his feet.

Maddy's tone hardened. "Not just us. All the families you tore apart...and Sarah."

At her name, his expression shifted sharply. The faint smile vanished, and his mouth tightened. He started to pace, slow at first, then faster, his shoes splashing in the shallow puddles along the path. Each turn brought him closer to the edge before he wheeled round again.

His voice cracked as he spoke. "She wasn't meant to die." He paused and took a breath. "They weren't meant to live. Fate doesn't forgive mistakes. Fate balances what we try to twist." His hands flexed at his sides, restless, unable to stay still.

"You killed them, Daniel," Maddy snapped, her voice rising over the wind. "That wasn't fate. That was murder, and you chose it." Her throat tightened and the words escaped before she could stop them. "Did you kill my dad too?"

His laugh cut through the rain, short and jagged. "Not every death is mine, Sergeant. Some people meet their end without me lifting a finger." He leaned a little closer to the edge, eyes fixed on her. "Maybe your father was one of those. Maybe fate wrote him off without my help."

His gaze locked on hers, a glimmer of cruelty sparking behind it. "You can't outrun it either. None of us can."

The words hit harder than the wind tearing at her coat. For a second her chest seized, the cliff path tilting beneath her boots. If he was lying, she couldn't prove it. If he was telling the truth, she was no closer to answers. Either way, her dad's death stayed in the grip of fate, just as Daniel wanted her to believe.

He spun on his heel, his face tight with pain and fury. "I pulled them back when they should have gone. I thought I was giving them something. A second chance. But all that happened is that Sarah was robbed from me! Don't you see? Fate always wins! It always takes! You can't cheat it!" His voice cracked, raw with years of grief twisted into something darker. "Every life I saved, every person who walked away... and she still died. She was taken from me anyway." His voice dropped at the last words, more broken than angry.

Maddy took a careful step forward, "Sarah was more than just how she died." She lowered her voice. "She was a woman with her own choices. She laughed, she lived, she argued. You're twisting her memory into a story she never agreed to."

Daniel barked out a short laugh, bitter and jagged. "You

think you knew her better than I did? You didn't see her in those last moments. The light leaving her eyes. That was my life ending with hers. And every time I pulled someone else back, I felt it all over again." His eyes glistened as he stared past Maddy at something only he could see. "Don't you understand? Letting them live was like spitting on her grave."

"You're wrong," Maddy pressed, her voice firm but calm. "She wouldn't want this. She wouldn't want you to do this to yourself or to others. You're turning her memory into a weapon."

Daniel Cross shook his head sharply, water flying from his hair. "No. No, I gave them the gift of survival, and they squandered it. They went back to their petty lives, their careless choices, while my Sarah is gone forever. Why should they be allowed what she never had?" His voice broke as he gestured wildly with one hand. "Why should they breathe while she's in the ground?"

Behind Maddy, Emily, and two armed officers moved slowly into position, their boots making soft sounds against the wet ground. Their jackets gleamed dark with rain. Weapons stayed low but ready, their eyes locked on the spiralling paramedic. The space closed inch by inch.

His eyes darted between them before snapping back to Maddy. "You can't stop it. Fate's already written. You'll lock me up, but you'll never change the truth. They weren't meant to live. I was only setting things right."

"Nothing was set right," Maddy answered, her tone hard as steel. "You stole from families. You stole their peace. And you've convinced yourself it was justice because you can't face your own grief."

His lips trembled, his face twisting. "Grief is all I have left."

His hand went into his coat. The movement was sudden

enough to draw a sharp intake of breath from Emily. He pulled out a knife, the steel glinting dull in the low light.

Immediately, the armed officers surged forward from their positions, breaking cover. "Knife! Weapon!" Their voices sharp and urgent, cutting through the wind. "Drop it! Drop the weapon now!"

Daniel's head snapped around, his eyes wide with shock as he registered the armed team. "You brought them?" His voice cracked with betrayal, the knife trembling in his hand. "You said you'd come alone!"

"I said I came," Maddy corrected steadily. "I never said alone."

His face twisted with fury and something like hurt. He raised the knife higher, the blade angled between them, his chest heaving harder now. His gaze darted between Maddy and the firearms officers, trapped.

Maddy raised one hand towards the firearms team without taking her eyes off Daniel. "Stand down. I've got this." Her voice was steady, commanding. She wanted him alive. She wanted him to face what he'd done, to stand in a courtroom and answer for every life he'd taken. Not to die here in a hail of bullets, escaping into some twisted martyrdom.

"Put it down, Daniel," Maddy said firmly, her stance unflinching. Her voice cut across the wind and rain with steady force.

His breathing grew ragged and his eyes darted towards the sea, then back to her. His grip tightened on the handle, knuckles stark white against the dark metal.

Maddy kept her eyes fixed on him, her voice level and steady, carrying enough authority to cut through the roar of the wind. "Daniel, if you believe in fate, then let it end here. But not with more blood on your hands."

His hand shook violently, the blade wavering as if it could

fly from his grip at any moment. He lifted it higher, his arm jerking between attack and surrender, then forced it back down an inch. His chest rose and fell sharply, each breath laboured, fogging in the cold air. His eyes darted between Maddy and the sea, desperate, uncertain, his face shifting rapidly between rage, despair, and something close to fear.

"Don't tell me what Sarah would have wanted," he snapped suddenly, voice cracking. "You didn't love her. You didn't hold her hand when they pulled her from that wreck." His throat tightened around the words, and the knife twitched upwards again. "You don't know what it's like to watch someone slip away, knowing it was supposed to be you instead."

Maddy raised her voice over the roar of the waves. "I know loss, Daniel. Most in this town do. But we don't take innocent lives to balance it. That isn't justice, that isn't fate, that's you choosing to hurt people."

Emily edged forward, boots careful on the wet path. Her voice was calm but projected clearly, trying to wedge into the crack Maddy had made. "You don't have to be alone, Daniel," she said. "It doesn't end with you staring at the sea. Let us take it. Let us carry it for you." She raised one hand, palm open, showing she carried no weapon. Her eyes never left his.

Daniel's shoulders trembled hard. He let out a sound, part groan, part sob, then staggered a half-step towards the edge as if the cliff itself was pulling him. "She was everything," he cried, the knife shaking in his hand. "And I have nothing. Every time I saved someone else, every time they walked away alive when Sarah didn't..." His voice cracked, raw with grief. "I see her death all over again. I see the moment I lost her, and I know I should have been the one who died, not her. How can I live with that?"

Maddy took another step forward, heart pounding, her voice rough but controlled. "By facing it. By accepting that

Sarah's gone and that you can't bring her back by punishing strangers. Put the knife down, Daniel. Don't let this end with you jumping or me watching another person die."

He looked at her, the fight draining from his eyes. He glanced at Emily, then back at Maddy, his grip loosening. "Maybe... maybe I was wrong," he whispered. Rain streaked down his face, mixing with tears. His arm dropped suddenly, the knife clattering loudly against the ground before bouncing against a stone and lying still.

The armed officers surged forward, boots pounding on the slick path. One swept the knife away with a heavy kick, the other closed on Daniel, seizing his arm and twisting it behind his back. The cuffs snapped shut with a hard metallic click. Daniel gave no resistance. His body sagged as they secured him, his head dropping, eyes fixed somewhere beyond Maddy as though he couldn't bear to meet her gaze.

Rain pelted down harder, plastering Maddy's hair across her face, soaking her jacket through to the skin. She stood frozen, every muscle rigid, her eyes locked onto the broken paramedic as he was dragged back from the cliff. His face was eerily calm now, emptied of everything, as though surrender had been the only path left to him. Each step he took with the officers looked stiff, mechanical, but inevitable. He never once looked back at the knife lying abandoned in the puddles.

Emily moved to Maddy's side, chest heaving from the adrenaline. Her breath caught before she spoke. "It's over, Mads."

Maddy gave the slightest nod, though the tension in her neck barely allowed it. Her eyes stayed on the churning waves below, the roar filling the silence that followed. Her jaw locked tight, her fists clenched, her body refusing to release the coil of energy and dread wound into it. The relief she should have felt never came; all she could feel was the tightness in her chest and the phantom weight of what might have happened if Daniel Cross had taken one more step forward.

* * *

Daniel Cross was escorted to the waiting vehicles, the officers keeping their grips firm. DI Harper walked past Maddy and, for once, said nothing. He placed one hand on her shoulder, brief but solid, before moving on. The look in his eyes was enough, a wordless acknowledgement that she had carried the case through when it could easily have broken apart weeks ago.

Up on the road above the cliffs, reporters had already gathered, their equipment glinting in the thin light just as the rain slowed and eased. Their microphones and cameras jutted out, voices calling for statements and questions. Some shouted her name, trying to get her attention. Maddy ignored them all. Among the group, Tom Denton stood a little apart, notebook in hand, his expression watchful. He didn't shout or push forward. He simply met her eyes across the distance and held them. A nod passed between them, silent, and heavy. She returned it, just briefly, before turning away. She could still feel his eyes on her back.

By the time she reached her car, the exhaustion she had been holding back finally flooded her. Every muscle ached, her clothes heavy with rain. Her chest felt tight, her throat dry, her head buzzing from all the hours of focus and confrontation. The drive home blurred into little more than wet roads, streaks of water on the windscreen, the occasional passing lorry sending up spray. Traffic lights and shopfronts slipped by without registering. She gripped the wheel tighter than necessary to keep herself steady.

She pulled up outside her mam's house, the familiar sight grounded her in a way nothing else could. The curtains in the front window were drawn back, the warm glow of the lamp inside spilling onto the street. She sat in the car for a long minute before opening the door, forcing herself out into the drizzle. Her shoes slapped against the pavement as she walked to the door.

Inside, Claire stood waiting, a blanket draped over her arm and two mugs already set on the table, steam curling into the air. She looked her daughter up and down without speaking, then stepped forward and wrapped the blanket around Maddy's shoulders, tucking it close as if she were still a child. She pressed a mug into her hands.

"Sit," Claire said quietly. "You need it."

Maddy sat heavily at the table, the chair creaking under her as she lowered herself down. She stared into the steam rising from her cup, the warmth reaching her face. Her voice cracked when she finally spoke.

"I got him, Mam."

Her mam came round the table, pulled out the chair beside her and sat close. She wrapped one arm around her daughter, firm and steady, and pulled her into a hug that Maddy didn't resist. "And now it's done," she said softly, brushing a damp strand of hair from Maddy's forehead.

Maddy leaned into the hug, the warmth steadying her. Claire's voice was quiet, careful. "Did he admit it? About your father?"

Maddy pulled back slightly, shaking her head. "He wouldn't say. Just...left it open. 'Maybe fate wrote him off without my help.'" She laughed bitterly. "Even at the end, he couldn't give me that."

Claire's hand tightened on her shoulder. "Then we'll never know for certain."

"No," Maddy said, her voice breaking. "We won't."

They sat in silence, the weight of that uncertainty settling between them like it always would. Her father's death would remain what it had always been: a question without an answer, a wound that would never fully heal.

Maddy closed her eyes for a moment, her shoulders loosening just enough to let the blanket fall further around her frame. The kettle clicked as it cooled, the only sound in the room and outside the rain kept on, rattling against the windows. Inside the Frost kitchen, there was silence, the kind that carried comfort as much as fatigue.

Chapter Twenty-Eight

Whitby woke under brooding skies, the kind that made the rooftops look flat and leached of all colour. Rain hung in the air but had not yet fallen. The station carried the usual Monday hum, phones ringing, keyboards clacking, voices kept to a steady level, but underneath it all was the weight of the investigation finally wrapped up. Daniel Cross was in custody. It was over, at last.

Maddy walked slowly through the corridor, a folder clutched against her chest. Her shoes sounded heavier than usual on the lino floor, each step dragging as her body decided to remind her it had been running on fumes for weeks. The sleepless night after his arrest had left her feeling hollow. She caught her reflection briefly in the glass panel of an office door, dark smudges beneath her eyes, skin pale, hair still damp from the drizzle outside. It was the look of someone who had carried too much for too long.

At her desk she pulled the final form from the folder, her statement written in the neat block handwriting she reverted to when she was exhausted. She read it once more, the words blurring together: the confession from Daniel, the arrest, the recovery of the weapon, and the statements from witnesses. Nothing dramatic. Just facts, stripped down as procedure demanded. She initialled the last page and slid it into the tray for completed reports. She knew she would only be in for half the day, Harper having told her to go home once the paperwork was done. The thought of leaving the building early felt unusual, as if she was stepping away too soon, but her body was grateful for it.

"Frost."

Harper's voice carried from his office doorway. He didn't bark it. Just said her name with a level tone that made everyone else in the incident room pause for a moment. He gave a brief nod and disappeared back inside.

Maddy pushed herself up and followed. His blinds were half closed, his desk neat apart from a cup of tea cooling by his elbow. He sat with both hands flat on the paperwork in front of him. He didn't tell her to sit, but she did, lowering herself into the chair opposite. Her shoulders ached, her arms heavy.

He looked at her for a long moment, then spoke. "You broke protocol. You took liberties with press access. You almost got yourself killed." The words came flat, measured, not accusatory but firm.

Maddy held his gaze. "Yes, sir."

A sigh left him. He leaned back in his chair, rubbing his jaw briefly. "But you were right." He reached for the file, tapped it once, then slid it across the desk. "The report says it was a team effort. We both know you carried it across the line."

Her throat felt tight, but she only gave a small nod. "Thank you."

Harper lifted his cup, realised the tea had gone cold, and set it down again. There was no handshake, no smile. Just a flicker in his expression, something close to respect, before he turned back to the paperwork. Maddy stood quietly and left him to it.

* * *

Outside, Whitby carried on as though nothing had happened. The harbour was busy with gulls screeching overhead, occasionally dive-bombing the tourists in waterproofs shuffling along the cobbles. The drizzle had returned, soft enough that most people ignored it. The smell of fish and diesel lingered in the breeze.

Maddy stepped onto Pier Road and pulled her coat tighter. She fished her phone from her pocket and checked her messages. One new text lit the screen.

Pleased you got your win. Let's chat soon. – Tom.

She read it twice, then locked the screen without replying. The words sat heavy in her pocket as she walked on, shoes clattering against the wet stones.

By the harbour railings, she paused, resting her forearms on the cold metal. A trawler was easing back into its berth, ropes thrown to men waiting on the quayside. She watched them move with the practised rhythm of people who knew the sea would punish any hesitation. The breeze tugged at her hair, damp strands sticking to her cheek. She let it clear her head, just for a moment. The immediate danger was over with Daniel in custody, but the noise in her chest hadn't stilled.

She stayed there until the cold bit into her fingers, then pushed herself upright and turned back towards home.

The drizzle had stopped by the time Maddy reached the house. In the small front garden, Claire was already at work with secateurs in hand, pruning the climbing rose that clung to the old brick wall. Maddy changed into her oldest jeans and a faded jumper and put on some gloves before kneeling in the soil to clear weeds from the flower bed. The earthy smell grounded her more than anything else had that day.

For a while, neither spoke. The snip of Her mam's secateurs and the rustle of pulled weeds were the only sounds. It felt almost normal, quiet, safe.

Claire straightened, brushing soil from her palms. "You're pulling too hard. You'll snap the roots if you're not careful."

Maddy gave a small huff. "Maybe I should stick to crime scenes. Less chance of killing something."

Her mam gave a short laugh, shaking her head, but didn't press. They worked side by side until the squeak of the garden gate made them both look up.

Jack stood there, waterproof jacket zipped to the chin, a faint smudge of oil marking his collar. He hesitated before speaking. "Didn't mean to interrupt," he smiled. "Just on my way down to the boats."

Maddy straightened slowly, tugging her gloves off. "You're not interrupting." She felt a flicker of surprise in her chest that warmed quickly, though she masked it with a neutral tone.

He stepped forward, the gate clicking shut behind him. "Well done, Mads," he said quietly, and pulled her into a brief hug that smelled faintly of salt and oil. When he stepped back, his expression was careful, unreadable.

Claire watched from her place by the rose bush, eyes flicking between them but saying nothing. Only the slight arch of her brow gave her away.

Jack tipped his head to her mam. "Hello, there, Claire. Right, I'd better get moving before the tide turns." He paused, then turned back to Maddy. "Listen, maybe when you've had a bit of rest we could go for a pint, or even grab some dinner. Just the two of us. You could use a break, and so could I."

Maddy felt her throat tighten, the words catching her off guard. She gave him a small smile. "Maybe I could, aye. Text me."

His eyes lingered on hers for a moment longer, warm and steady. "Good. I'll be in touch then."

And then he was gone, boots crunching back down the street. The gate shut with a clink, the sound carrying in the still garden. Maddy stood still for a moment, gloves dangling from one hand, before crouching back to the weeds. The warmth of his hug lingered, unsettling but not unwelcome. For a second, Daniel Cross' words about her dad pressed back into her thoughts, the suggestion that fate had stolen him without help. She pushed the memory down, digging harder at the soil as if the earth itself might anchor her. Claire's look lingered on her, curious but quiet, but she chose not to comment, letting the moment hang in the damp air.

* * *

As early evening settled in and the light thinned across the town, Maddy walked alone towards the memorial plaque outside the station entrance. The building stood quiet behind her, most of the team gone home, the windows glowing faintly in the gathering dusk. Rain began to fall, steady and cool, but she didn't bother with an umbrella. She was a Whitby woman, after all. Her hair clung damp to her forehead as she stood at the familiar spot.

The plaque was slick with rain, her father's name clear against the metal. She crouched and placed a smooth white pebble at the base, its underside marked with a tiny hand drawn x. Only she and her dad would have understood the symbol. Simple. Private. Hers.

Her father's case file would remain open, technically. No confession. No evidence linking the damned paramedic definitively to that hit-and-run three days after the first accident. Just Daniel's careful ambiguity and her own suspicions. She'd put a serial killer behind bars, saved future lives, brought justice for Andy, Sophie, Peter, Tessa, and the others. But for her father? Nothing. No closure. No certainty. Just the hollow ache of not knowing.

She supposed that was its own kind of fate.

She stood slowly, her fingertips brushing the edge of the plaque once before she turned away.

The walk towards the harbour was instinctive, her feet carrying her through familiar streets without thought. The wind was sharp off the sea, carrying spray from the waves that broke against the stone pier. Rain fell harder now, soaking through her coat, but she welcomed the cold.

She stood at the water's edge with the sound of the sea filling the silence. Words formed slowly, steady in her head. People talk about fate like it is a straight line. But I've seen what happens when someone believes it too much, when they try to force it. My dad didn't die for fate. He died for a choice, to pursue the truth, no matter the cost.

Her chest tightened, but she let the thought settle. That's what I will do too.

The rain soaked her shoulders, ran cold down her arms, but she didn't move for a long time. The waves crashed against the harbour wall, relentless and unchanging. Finally, she turned away from the water's edge, the roar of the sea in her ears. For once, the storm was behind her.

Continue DS Maddy Frost's Whitby return in Book Two here: Fate's Debt

Fate's End

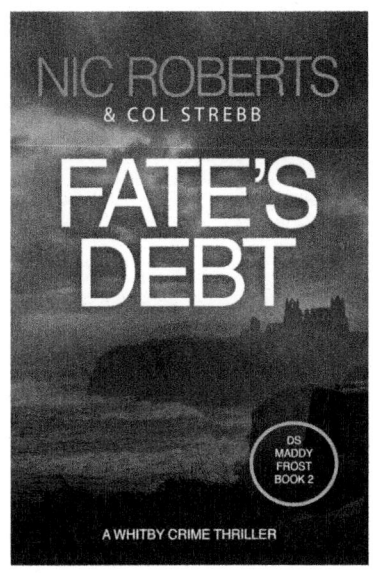

Love to read Detective Thrillers?

Join my Newsletter to be the first to hear about New Releases and ARC opportunities.

http://eepurl.com/hskzML

About Nic Roberts

I've always had a passion for writing stories and loved being able to create a world and have my characters live inside it. Being able to do this has been a dream come true, and I'm so grateful that you could join me on this journey.
I live in the United Kingdom with my Husband and four children, who keep me busy and who I wouldn't ever be without.
I hope you enjoy reading my books, and please feel free to join me on social media.

mrsrobertswrites@hotmail.com

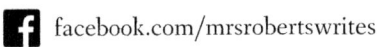 facebook.com/mrsrobertswrites

Printed in Dunstable, United Kingdom